Girl

Maria Straw -Çinar

Girl

ISBN 978-1-9161545-3-7

For Iris

Contents

EINSTEIN TIME

I need to start tonight. Start to get it all down. Now I have this pen I am mightier than the sword. It's yellow cold out here in this beautiful bald desert and the stars that shine the brightest look like numbers in the sky. 369. The outline of the three Berbers on their camels is etched into the sky as your small face lights up and your tiny fingers reach for the moon. They are coming to you my love wrapped in your swaddling clothes. Your life will be better than mine. Simpler with no hearts to tear out. You will be free. Free. Sex. Nein.

Tis Time.

I can only remember in bursts. I can't remember punctuation even though I was a teacher many moons ago. 36 to be precise. When I remember I write it down. Sometimes I get lost and there is no order to things in my mind's eye but if I write it down I start to see things in close-up. Sometimes I burn it. It's a bit like the myth of the Minotaur. The God's cursed Theseus with the spell of forgetting and he couldn't remember if he should put up a white sail to signal he was alive so the black sail remained signalling he was dead. This one error led to many more deaths. Will I send out the wrong sign. Only time will tell. That tell-tale time.

I suppose you think because I'm a girl I give a glossy shit about how much I weigh and what I look like. Well this ain't that kind of story so you can stop reading now. I haven't seen a mirror in a year. Only my shadow outlined on the sand. I read the Beauty Myth and frankly I agree. I never read Jane Austen though and don't intend to. I've seen it on telly. I get the idea. Things were different then. Now we have the vote and brains. Big huge pulsating open minds. Don't get me wrong. We always had them but now some of us are using them and hell. Everyone's scared to shit.

I was a tomboy but seems just like yesterday a smelly old French guy on the train rubbed his dick on my leg and breathed in ecstasy. He had to get his kicks that way. It was close to rape but don't worry I've been much closer. Violence is always with us though I don't remember seeing much in Jane Austen.

You may wonder how I knew the guy was French. Well I was living in Paris at that time so most people were. I went there coz I like the cups they serve hot chocolate in and the way my Dad and I would bagsy buy the baguette in the morning when I was little. My Dad. He's not French. He's amazing. People are his champagne. That's what he wants on his gravestone. He's so damn wonderful it kills me. I've never met anyone like him and the bad thing is I probably never will.

Anyways. That's U.S English with the s. I like that. Anyways where do I begin. I wanna tell you about everything but like the Nepalese I'm afraid you'd steal my soul. I haven't spoken for years. Not out loud. I like words. Language. So much. Really. Where I am there are no seasons. Just sky. And sand. I want to tell you about the summer before last and I need to begin with the one before. Hot as a roasting cracked chestnut and full of surprises like a Catherine Wheel you should never go back to. But we always do. Go back. Don't we. But this time thing gets me. I like Gertrude Stein because everything she writes is in the present continuous. Like the way they speak in India.

She is coming this train she is coming to you in many minutes.

I love that. Presentness. I am writing about things and I am beginning and ending in the summer. Remember I was a girl. Not a woman. You're only a woman if you have a baby. No matter how old you are. I was a tomboy. Still am. But they don't know that. I have curves like Monroe and piercing blue eyes that light up lives. So I'm told. In fact one not-so-old old guy reckons I'm sister of the sands. That's a desert thing. That's where I am. I could be a girl but something in my head keeps trying to tell me I am a woman.

But inside-out I'll never be an adult. Though sometimes I used to pretend or they'd of said I was mad. No they would have said. Yes. I remember that. Anyways I'm going to turn myself inside out to write this. I hope you appreciate it. It's real. You need to listen though coz one thing I hate is people who don't. Listen. You say something and they just railroad over your words like a truck full of petroleum hollering past a dying earth portent. Really rain on your parade. I know the yellow brick road is long but I think we should stay on it. But there ain't room for bores on it or deafo blabber mouths. Those chosen ones who won't shut the fuck up. I can listen. That's why people like me. It's simple. I used to teach. English as you can see from my cursed punctuation. I've taught just almost every nationality one way or the other. I could list them but I won't. Just imagine the world. A globe. I have a little one. Just the size of a grapefruit and I like how it feels in my hands. Imagine all those different people in different places and me.

IRELAND

The summers and what lies between. The summer is beginning in the green Celtic land and is never-ending in the desert. Along the way I've been led into temptation and plenty of evil's been delivered. Yet I still love. The Emerald Isle. The land of fairies and scary sinsoaked monsters with druid circles and burial grounds and rounds and rounds. The garden. Like a teddy bear. One step. Two step. Tickle you under there.

Blacked out. Blank space. The desert. Pure wipe. Bluebell childhood memories return and the blue-faced cherry-blood choking fades to horizon gazing.

Space.

I hear silence. I love that.

The problem seems to be my open-mind.

OPEN

Open doors. Not shut. Not closed. Unlocked. Unbolted. Unlatched. Ajar. Unsecured. Wide open. Agape. Gaping. Yawning.

My face looks like an open road. Unobstructed. Unblocked. Clear. Passable. Navigable.

So open this mind of mine. I can't close it at night. I ask queer questions. I want to know. I don't like pretending I know everything. I don't. Like Socrates didn't but this was not a Greek thing. Apart from the tragedy and the Minotaur myth. It was life imitating art and how dare it. I was playing the Lady of the Manor. Double dare. I feel so funfunny when I play a lady coz it makes me realize. Love. I'm not one. Kiss. I don't mind or anything it just really tickles me tight inside. Or promise? So I was playing a lady in Sam's version of

Chekov's The Cherry Orchard. The one where they can't pay the bills so all the trees get cut down. It's sad. Chopping down perfectly good trees. I was The Lady of the Manor who fritters her money away in Paris. In a garret. Sam. He's great. Almost as great as my Dad. He's always chopping up classical plays then sticking his name on them. The thing with this play. We did it in a disco in Roscommon. The mild mild West. Strange as hell with crates for seats. The Irish. The few who came. They loved it. I was on the radio and everything and the old guy after bought me a Guinness and told me I was Chekov. He liked the way I played with my sweet wrapper nervously when I lost the orchard. I hadn't done that before and I liked it too.

I went to Paris after touring Ireland. A leprechaun clutching a baguette. Mr Benn style. Slipping through borders in seconds. Now you see me. Now you don't. After the strangulation. The strangled English girl and her artichoke heart. Opened sesamed bun. Not Celtic. But English. I thought I would move. Build bridges. All that hopeful-hippy I'm so lippy sugary-shit.

Only it's not shit.

We have to start somewhere and now Einstein's shown us that time is relative we may as well start with the strangulation. Besides my mind was travelling so fast that night that I was definitely seeing stars bending round time. We all see things from different angles and the faster you go the smaller things become. EinSteintime I call it in honour of Gertrude Stein who was big but understood that small things are important. Like the here and now. I never did Physics but I know about time. I know it is not straight. I just know it.

Beckett used to have fits of depression on his visits to Ireland so he moved to Paris. Hemingway or Hem or Tatie as his wife called him said that if you are lucky enough to have lived in Paris as a young man then wherever you go for the rest of your life it stays with you for Paris is a moveable feast. He was so pigeon-shit right. Paris rocks.

But unlike Beckett I was obsessed with going to Ireland. The magical mystery tour and the Celtic tales pulled me across the waters. Sam and I we took the boat together and he told me tales of his life and his shady past. His eyes looked as though they had seen it all. We drank Cork gin right through the night and I drove us down the ramp onto the land as the sun shone and palm trees glistened so just what was Beckett so down about. Driving past the port ravenously hunting out an Irish breakfast. We devour the food to soak up all the gin and lie on the beach. Sam and I decide to swim. I tell him that I am a dolphin and the great thing about Sam is that he knows what I mean. Mannis and the old twinkling eyed man swimming free and innocent in the frothy foamy Irish sea.

His grey bald head god-like and noble to me. The old man and the sea. Soon to be free. We dry ourselves in the sun not caring about the sand. Sam has made a picnic of his favourite crab meat along with Wexford's biggest spring roll. We feast on the crabmeat. A feast to die for and stare out at the sea. He is my nemesis this twinkly eyed soulman. Back in the car we travel through Ireland with old gypsy carts blocking the road. I drop Sam in the bogland of Boyle and drive to Dublin through the expectant Irish night with the stars winking at me. I am full of glitter and promise. Skin-tingling open hearted me.

Dublin was wet after sun-scorched Wexford. Wandering through the streets running my lines over in my head. I walked into a show with two Irish actors telling tales of comedy and macabre. I preferred the macabre. The Hell Fire Club where the proprietor sets fire to an unwanted customer by dousing him with whisky and flicking the match. The legends are based on a place up in the Dublin mountains where nothing grows. I sat there next to a dance teacher with pink and gold tights. I loved her for those. She told me there were serial killers on the loose. In Ireland. Killing young women like myself. Her word 'women'. Not mine.

After the cinders and whisky were cleared away from the night at The Hell Fire Club and Dracula had bled some necks the actor with the fanged teeth told us a true story. The Harcourt Street Murders about a jealous lover who dismembers his girlfriend and only gets three years. After which he moved to South Africa and became a politician. Murderous love release us.

Anyday now.

Released into the street rain. I walk to my digs. Digging. Keep Digging. A truth truffle in truffle bare rooms. A woman's refuge was the only place I could find. A hiding place for bruised wives wrapped up in greasy fish n' chip men's hands. Awaiting pick up from the B and B for the drugged and destitute. Not that I was a battered fish wife. Not Me. Not Never. But it was the only cheap room in town and anyways I wouldn't wanna stay in luxury 5 star mini barblues. I might lose touch with my soul. The lady of the house doused me with greasy pig flesh. Blood sausage-sweet pudding with chicken foetus and tomato sauce. Fat and kindness. And the children. God Bless Them. Set to work.

Where ya from?

Whats ya name?

Do you believe in God?

No.

Their little faces looked so confused. So hopeful. So I said. As people do. When they don't want to feel bare-boned alone.

Well yes a personal God. Good. I believe in good.

but saw their faces wide-eyed bemused.

How can you not believe in God?

Young.

Everyone believes in God.

I felt myself floating into the oily emerald ether and all anyone wants is certainty so I said it. For their soulssake.

OK. Just kidding. I do.

Some say I look like an angel and maybe that's coz my grandfather was a preacher man. I wasn't brought up in Eton. I was eaten and brought up. In The Salvation Army. So I know all about saints and sinners. My grandfather used to preach at Hyde Park corner chaining my Nan up in seven chains of sin. He led her through the park on a horse as he bellowed his war cry:

COME AND SEE THE WOMAN UNCHAINED!

UNCHAIN YOURSELF FROM SIN!

The Salvation Army is an Army at war with evil. Crusaders against harm. A proper war on terror. I was brought up as a young soldier to fight evil. I marched and banged my tambourine in the fight for goodness. It is organised like the real Army but the weapon is love and those kind of bullets pierce the flesh in unusual ways. Sometimes it can hurt a hell of a lot more. My auntie was a Colonel and my grandmother was a Brigadier. All soldiers are like actors sent into battle for a lost cause. That's the beauty of their doomed passion.

Do you believe in God?

He asked the priests to take care of the little ones but some of them cared for them in unusual ways.

What!?

Nothing.

I believe in sleep. I retreated from the mini-priests to my room. Double triple locked bolted from the vicious wife-beating men. Inside myself I curled up. Foetus-full and ready to start anew. Sleeping through all the shouting and banging and pain. The sorrowful husbands come to drag their wives back to domestic bliss with a kiss.

For thirteen hours.

I reached for the soul-switch. Sleep. Chief comforter in life's feast. Sleep that knits up the ravell'd sleeve of care. The death of each day's life. Balm of hurt minds. Great nature's second course. Sleep. Coma-comfort click-trick metamorphosis from teaching English as an eFing Language to actress with starring role. Actor. It's a better word. Performer. Player. Dramatic artist. Thespian. Thespis who spoke out from the crowd. Trouper. Tragedian. Leading man-woman. If you say actress just sounds like you're a barking Blanche du Bois mad woman who can't be seen in bright light and often relies on the kindness of strangers. That's not me. No.

Light. Definition: the natural agent which emanates from the sun. An intensely heated object stimulates sight. The medium or condition in which this is present and in which vision is possible.

WHITE washing ablutio. Baptisma or the soul anima released at death is reunited with the body and resurrects the many colours. The peacock tail leads to the one white colour that contains all colours.

Glimpsed in a rainbow.

This is the silver moon condition. Almost day-break but not quite. The desert light where nothing grows. Perfect blue light opens wide my eyes hidden shut.

I look.

I and nothing.

I and land.

Wash away all other hands.

Under the date palm tree hands touch deep my back. My skin breathes in. Out. Now all I see is nothing but this desert light. Tunnelling inside sight. My eyes white stars ahead look deep into the crystal ball past as the sun brain-clears me.

White hands.

I am seeing the cherry blossom and I feel the mouldy Emerald hands squeezing tighter and tighter.

White blossom.

Towards The Cherry Orchard I go.

THE CHERRY ORCHARD

In preparation for our parts we bring our dressing up clothes to Coolatin House and look at slides of Ireland in the 1970's. I hear what the English did. Stealing the best land and houses for their greedy selves. The Anglo-Irish Lords and Ladies lording it over the little people. Champagne for their real English friends and real pain for their sham Irish shamrock friends. I spend my time drifting around the old house we will perform in. Getting into character. So many characters to remember. I was playing a Lady. I remember that house very well. That day I felt like a child again. Free to play and stay forever and never realize the time.

I read Vogue in my pink gown plopping cherries in my mouth to add to the utter decadence of it all and the Irish characters donned boots and farming clothes to show they are of the land. Maddie pulls the frumpy country clothes over her attractive body and put on her deepest thick Paddy accent. She makes me laugh. She plays my daughter. My daughter.

Paysants. The people of the land. Literally translates as the earthy ones.

It is a land man who takes the Orchard from me. The peasants made good and rich. The Celtic tiger roaring its revenge on the fading mad aristocrats.

I'm not tick or anyfing Mrs Ranelagh. Says the Irish actor.

No 'h' s there. The play clearly displays just how the sins of our ancestors will be visited upon us as the orchard is chopped down around my ears.

I feel something like the hand of death on me.

I end up rotting away in my garret. Begging for money for drink. In the end I leave for Paris. In the play and in real life.

MADDIE THE GOODGIRL WITCH

After staying with Maddie and her thirteen cats my luck was running out. I was losing my Cherry Orchard every night so of course I needed to let off steam. Making Chekov Irish is bound to have repercussions. The lines said it all.

I feel something like the hand of death on me.

Huge hands there waiting in the wings. Greedy hands and history had planted the seeds. The same seeds that burst and flourish and open out this lushland before me. After two weeks rehearsing how to tell our playstory we earned ourselves a break. Lying under the sun looking out at the hills.

The 13 cats nap and lick my feet.

Maddie's icecold blacksyrup surprise on a hazyhot yawning morning. A tall glass tower of delight from my hangover night. So good inside when out of the trueblue sky someone makes you so high. A surprise. Something you never expected.

Surprise: 1. the action or an act of attacking or seizing a place unexpected, attack on or capture.

2. the action or an act of coming upon a person unawares, a sudden attack.

My first surprise of the day. Maddie glass in hand standing beside me and offering me the coolest blackshower I have ever swallowed. I know it's good for me. The glorious sun-kissed hills of Wicklow. All calm apart from the occasional gunshot signifying another rabbit's release from this mortal coil and the humhum of the lawnmower man who is Maddie's man. Now Maddie of the thirteen cats fame was my daughter that summer. Fictional. In the play. Not in Real life. A magical fairy girl. Not woman. She has no babies. Only cats. We had become friends after sharing a freezing cold bed and a glass or ten of our cups which both runneth over with warmlove. Us. Inside the warmnight lock-in playing each other's strings to fever all through the night pitch. Purely platonic. I'm afraid. Though maybe The Strangler didn't know that. There were many things I liked about her. She had built herself a home in the woodforest. A remote cabin in the hills.

A mystery. A madwoman. A witch.

Witchcraft Witchery. Sorcery. Black art/magic. Necromancy. Wizardry. Occultism. The occult. Sortilege. Thaumaturgy. Wonderworking.

Just a few hundred years ago thousands of wonderworkers were killed.

They say the water won't keep a witch in. If you float you're a witch and condemned to be hanged. If you drown you're not a witch but you're dead anyway. Clever stuff.

We all kill what we fear. Tread on a slug. Kill the wasp before it stings. Kill the spider. Kill the light. Kill love. Kill our good selves. For each man kills the thing he loves. Womankind.

But Maddie was the good witch Glenda soft voice fairy god-girl of the enchanted wood. Under her wing-wand nothing could go wrong.

Except it did.

When I met Donal. The boyfriend. The Strangler who tried to throttle me throatless. On our first meeting. Those first impressions keep you guessing.

Quite an affair I can tell you. It'll get you all choked up.

Now then.

THE STRANGULATION

Inside the Irish pumping pub smoked night. I walk pale blue strong-blond Viking drinking farmer-finger looking good. The sculptor took a shine to me held out a line to me that I did not catch. Should have said I was Celt. Me Mannis raising hell in the clan banned session. Maddie is excited to introduce me to her boyfriend. Her very own Dagda and she the Goddess of Boyne. He is an enormous burly man like a giant from a fairy tale with a big old laugh that defies you to disagree. He shakes my hand which feels crushed in his huge meaty paws. Like the Pigman's. I should have known.

Great to meet ya. You've got fine bones. You must be Swedish.

No.

Scandinavian.

No. I'm English.

Nah. Ya can't be English.

Yes. I am.

Your neck it's just right for sculpting.

No really you have a beautiful neck.

Are you Scandinavian?

Do you get naked in the cold ice? Could you go down on me twice?

Common complements spewing from this hot-blooded Celtictiger bearmouth. Sculptor slash Artist slash Musician slash Bon viveur.

Slashed

He. Blarney King kissed that eloquent stone too many times. He. Extolling the virtues of my neck. So juicyripe for artistic abuses.

Extol: Praise. Praise highly. Praise to the skies. Sing the praises of. Applaud. Acclaim. Pay tribute to. Laud. Eulogize about. Exalt. Commend. Congratulate. Celebrate. Compliment. Glorify. Panegyrize. Magnify.

Are you Celtic? Can I sculpt your neck?

It's just right for fingering.

The Lough land so immense in its changing blue black sky. A temper flash stashed away for those oh so many Irish rainy days. A climate moody and beautifully bruised where people lick their wounds with homespun black treacle that'll smooth away those painful Paddy potato-thick edges but glue you to a past of pain in the rain and here it comes again. Don't forget your manners Mannis. Let the nice man touch your neck.

You must be Celtic or something you can't just be English

The word English was spat out. Salt in his coffee instead of sugar.

Slurring liquor-led lust.

Really the most beautiful neck I have ever seen.

You must be Celtic!

and lo!

You can't be English

And behold !

The national anthem starts to play and all the bruise boozed rinsed out revellers stand to attention.

Fucking English. You fucking English bastards. My Auntie carried guns in her knickers because of you fucking English bastards...

English. Angled. Acute whore thorn in his side. And I Mannis screaming over the music fighting my bloodsmeared corner defending my time. It was not my fault.

BUT I was born in 1970...

I was brought up in a multicultural comprehensive class-crushed Pink Floyd sausage-machine brick in the wall Socialist school.

So proud of themselves. The oppressed.

YOU SPEAK WITH THE CROOKED VOICE OF HISTORY.

He roars**.**

My drunken loose gaping mouth spilling cavernous truths. Locked away in sobriety and now so happy to be aloud out to party.

I HAD NOTHING TO DO WITH….

The sins of our ancestors…

My neck as long as a giraffe's. Those gangly gingergiants born with an extra heart pump to send the blood up up into their brain. My ancestors on the road to Mandalay! Tipperary! Bombay ! Happy and gay. Here to stay. Come what may. The Trouser People laughed at by enclosed Burmese Brassnecks. The Giraffe women of Padaung. Necks in heavy brass coils. Elongated coz it looks better that way.

And it's a long way to Tipperary…

This angry Giant is as high as a kite and no beanstalk in sight.

A long way to go…

Tonight I need that extra pump.

Breathe.

The National Anthem plays.

Who will be the first through the Gap of Danger….?

And just remember curiosity killed the cat.

Do they always play the National Anthem at the end of the…?

A couple of seconds and litres of wine-swine later his hands flew at me. Squeezing. Hard. Shocked. Heart-stopped blood-lines spinning beer-barn around me. Viking strength fading. Fight Mannis. Fight. Enormous hands clasped around my once beautiful neck. Wildean words. Each man destroys the thing he loves. Maddie's squeeze. Squeezing the life out of Mannis Poor aged 29 and…a… quarter. Aged years in seconds.

IF YOUR FUCKING AUNTIE WAS CELEBRATING HER FUCKING SEVENTY-FIFTH BIRTHDAY YOU'D WANNA FUCKING CELEBRATE THIS COUNTRY'S FUCKING SEVENTY-FIVE YEARS OLD AND MY FUCKING AUNTIE WAS HIDING GUNS IN HER FUCKING KNICKERS FROM YOU FUCKING ENGLISH BASTARDS….

BUT I WAS BORN IN 1970...

Never answer back to a clanman, little girlsworld.

The hands hard and clannish wrapped firm round my giraffeneck…. Tighter…Tighter.

Slap me with your belt.

Squeeze me till I'm Celt

FI ! FIE! FO! FUM!

I SMELL THE BLOOD OF AN ENGLISH WOMAN.

Can't talk. Hands drop to my side. Doll-like and stupid laughable bloody lust. Lock in. Locked in. Breathe in. Out. Can't breath.

HELP!

Was. At. Hand… from Patrick. Skin and bone. Weak. Helpless. Terrified of the Great God of Stone. Patrick the brave put a hand on the sculptors' shoulder. A street beggar tapping the feet of the cityslickers shiny shoe. A ladybird diverting a dinosaur. Like the twin towers down in a New York minute. Survival of the fittest. The strongest. The drunkest. The angriest.

Patrick called security who bounced over. Wild eyed drunks everywhere.

Drunken haven.

Here we go…

DRUNK the past of drink. That parasite past. Like that Catherine Wheel you should never go back too. But we always do. Go back. Back there. The hope that we may get it going again spark it into life where we can spin and burn and wheel and laugh drink drink for tomorrow we shall die… But alas says poisoned Parker. We never do.

Drunk as a lord. Blind drunk. Dead drunk. Intoxicated. Inebriated. The worse for drink. Under the influence. Tipsy. Soused. Gin-soaked. Befuddled. Maudlin. Sottish. Toping. Bibulous. Crapulent.

Catherine Wheel drunk.

Tight. Tiddly. Squiffy. Merry. Happy. Woozy. Pie-eyed. Half-seas-over. Three sheets to the wind. Under the table.

HAVENT YOU HAD ENOUGH YET?

NOOOOO!

Out of it. Legless. Plastered. Smashed. Paralytic. Sloshed. Blotto. Blitzed. Lit up hey! Hey! There's old Catherine!

DRINKING UP TIME! Time for bed so you can wake up to make the munitions in the morning to stop Jerry Paddy Tommy…

Canned. Bevvied. Stewed. Pickled. Tanked-up. Soaked. Bombed. Liquored up. Tired and emotional. Steaming.

Sober.

I'm so so sorry so fucking sober sorry.

And the Catherine Wheel is nailed deeper and deeper into that wooden fence of your past.

I see people everywhere beady-eyed like flies around shit. The bouncers bounce them away in random piles all over the village.

Rushed out by Maddie like the president after an assassination attempt shouting and stunned breathing again in out in out. Maddie now could see her man in all his rage and glory. Strong as an ox. Boxing his corner against the enemy within.

Thank you Patrick who had been telling me that Jim Morrison was really alive and that his coffin in Père Lachaise was full of sand. Had it not been for his intervention. Weak as he was. The Anglo-Irish stew would have erupted spilling and spewing me into my volcanic coffin. Full of lava me.

Shipped home.

At least it would cure my fear of flying.

In the car. Safe and breathing. Lung-stung breath.

Breathe.

Lungs:The respiratory organ which brings air into contact with the blood in many vertebrates occurring usually in pairs.

Woman and man occurring usually in pairs.

Maggie and Donal. A pair. The sculptor boyfriend with the artistic temperament 52 and I don't know how many halves got into a fight with me for being English. He was certain I was Scandinavian at first. Anything. Danish. Dutch. Anything but English and had I thought quicker I would have said this.

My father swears to me that if we dug up Robert the Bruce's grave in Scotland and matched his DNA with my saliva, hell, we'd be Celtic royalty.

I have a feeling Donal wouldn't understand. Fishing for the Celt in me like a diver searching for lost treasure in a filthy murky sea. That sea was England and the filth in his eye was me.

The sins of our ancestors are being visited upon us.

My line. Art and life and breath slowly returned.

I feel something like the hand of death on me.

I can hear her calling.

For what we are about to receive may the Lord make us truly thankful. Omen.

The Banshee… A wild haired woman combing her hair and screaming. Screaming bluemurder. Screaming the deathscream. Keening screaming women sitting over the corpses pulling out their hair. Helping the mourners to weep. Weeping is good. Crying. Wailing. Sobbing. Bawling. Shedding tears. Though I didn't. Not then. Fear is stone whitedeadness. I had it then and I have had it before with the Pig Man. I'll tell you about him.

Are you still there?

SINS OF OUR ANCESTORS

Sam meets me the next day and apologises on behalf of his countrymen. He starts telling me about a play he has written involving the poet Yeats and the revolutionary Maud Gonne. He says he wants to show me the Castle of Heroes where Yeats and Maud were to live in their spiritual marriage. We take the boat across the waters of Lough Key as Sam tells me stories of brave Maud. A revolutionary heroine who fought the British and inspired Yeats to write beautiful poetry. She had no second Troy to burn. She said she could not have sex because it made her shriek like a tortured pig and she carried a gun in her boot. As the mist descends over their Castle of Heroes Sam asks me to play this towering goddess from Irish history. To be a real heroine not just an idea on ink and paper. I will play her. It would be good to be a hero. For more than one day.

Beauty like a tightened bow.

Maud. Now then. She believed in the Tuatha De Danaan. She was always astral travelling. Sometimes I think like her. When my hair is red and my spirit strong. The Tuatha De Denaan. You and I need to know who they are.

The translation of *Tuatha Dé Danann* as "peoples of the goddess Danu" is necessarily imprecise. Old Irish *tuath* (plural *tuatha*) means "people, tribe, nation"; and *dé* is the genitive case of *día*, "god, goddess, supernatural being, object of worship".

Maybe not all that but you can see that they are pretty special beings full of light and intelligence. I may be one or a descendent of one. The Irish thought Maud was a goddess. They were tiny compared to her. Her hair was a majestic red. She fought tooth and nail to protect them from the bloody English smashing up all their houses. A vision rising from the stinking bog surrounded by butterflies.

Hair flaming like the red desert here.

Some days the sand is yellow. Other days it's orange and golden but today it is deep red like Maud's hair. I pull my hair to my mouth to suck it. It is the colour of the sun. I run my finger through the tiny grains of sand and divide it in to two roads. Two paths. I then add a third. Two but in the three we merry be.

May the road rise up to meet you.

Sam and I row back to the mainland and drive to see some burial grounds. I admire the majestic colours of the hills. The sky is moody and violent. Alive. Shifting but constant. Tumbling travellers we pull up at a pub where the clock goes backwards and an old man with big open-toed sandals tells us of fairies and leprechauns up in the hills. We ask him the way. He sends us further down deep into Bog country. Left at Katie Lavin's bar. Drive on for a mile past the Green Man and turn left for Gurteen then straight onto Ballymoat past the Donkey trail and just after the pub is the burial ground. Carrowkeel. A whole topography controlled by drink. Stories told by the little people. The fairies speak to me. Maybe they stole my child. My magical fairy girl. A lot of tales started with the big Daddy man.

DAGDA

Dagda. The Great big father of Ireland. He had a living oak harp called Uaithne which caused the seasons to change in their order.

The Uaithne played three types of music.

the music of sorrow

the music of joy

and the music of dreaming

<u>Music of Joy</u>

Once upon a time there was a gigantic mound like a pregnant belly or a giant tortoise. Inside the mound was a beautiful mansion beyond compare.

The first owner of the mansion was Elcmar the Druid, the consort of the Goddess Boann, the River Boyne. One day while Elcmar was away the Dagda appeared and wooed the Goddess Boann and they lay together and conceived a child. So that her husband would not know of their infidelity the Dagda magically caused nine months to pass in one day and thus Aongus Og was born on the same day he was conceived. Then the Dagda took possession of the mound and lived there for many years. Aongus grew up to become the God of Love of the Túatha Dé Danann, and is always associated with birds, especially swans.

I will always be associated with pink flamingos. I watch them land here in the desert and drink from the oasis. I can draw them. When I look at them for too long I feel invisible. They stand on one very thin leg. Like me. One-legged fragility in this three-legged race.

During the Dagda's reign at Brú na Boinne the place was

associated with magic and wonder. One day Aongus went to his father and asked for possession of the mound for a day and a night, to which the Dagda agreed. When he came back the next day, his son informed him that since all eternity is made up of day and night, the Dagda should give Aongus the mound for ever. And so it became the Brú of Aongus Og.

Three sons of three kings were advised to go to the Brú and fast for three days, after which they were rewarded with land, wives and wealth. In early mythology the mound/womb is a place of conception and birth. The associations with death and funerals come from later Christian writings.

The Music of Sorrow

My Christian Angled time changing it to death.

Three kings will come to cut out my heart.

A Desert Rose will be born and she will spend three days in a stone tomb and emerge reborn.

It is folklore.

Almost biblical.

But a girl this time.

Music of dreaming

3 x 3 is 9. Dagda The Irish God passed 9 months in one day. Today could be yesterday and tomorrow. All eternity is day and night. The mound is conception and birth.

A magical child will be born in the middle of winter.

I am like Angus men call me young

I am the sunlight in the heart

Moonlight in the mind

I am the light at the end of every dream

I will make you immortal
For my Palace opens into the Gardens of the Sun

There are some words that are crystal clear. Even here in the death desert. I can still hear the music of dreaming.

So I came here when the killing started. I came here in the end too. Maybe I have always been here. It was always calling me. The wilderness. The desert where I met my prince. It is always here I come back to. I live with the Berber woman. They are taking care of me now.

Berber from *Imazighen* (singular: *Amazigh*), meaning 'free people'.

They don't think I am strange. I don't think they think I am in hiding. They don't see the world in the same way. They know I write a lot then burn it up on the fire while they dance. They laugh and hug me. They do not write their language. They just speak. I never speak. I only write. That way nothing can change. We have our own language. The women are kind but some of the men can get too excited. Sexually I mean. Nothing new there. Sometimes the tourists come and I hide away with the Berber women. No-one notices me but I have to be careful. Especially when I hear their drumming. I need to dance. It drives me wild. The burning fiery danger that I hold inside me comes out sometimes. Especially when I dance.

Fighting broke out last night after I danced to the Berber drums. The heavy drum sound coming from the desire to make noises in the eerie silence. Banging and crashing. Noise is always with us. Like violence. You only realize the beauty when it's not there. Like peace. The drumming. A way of reaching out into nothingness. A sharing of rhythm and need for sexual pulses. Living pulse of the blood. Running through all our bodies. Fi fie fo fum I smell the blood of an English woman. I danced last night. A dance that raised the towers of our future to bursting spurting white creamy salty-teared glory but our future said no. The boys were angry and the girl retreated and hid in her lair. Licking her wounds and punished for letting and then not letting go. Perverting the course of nature.

Like sensimilia. The female hashish plant is kept apart from the male to avoid the buds. No-one gets high on the buds. Without the male they yearn and burn and produce the sweetest grass juice known to any Jamaican smokesman. Burning up the desire. Gone in a puff of smoke.

Outside the desert hut the drum beats beat the weak Western bodies. All tangled up inside. They sit passive husks of their stardust selves. They hear something through their wax-blocked electronic ears but they just cannot move. Stymied shells. Cannot find their île déserte. All but Me Mannis. I crack.

I stand broken shell of English teatime. Stymied preserved jam reserve. Pieces of shrapnel fall around me and outside runs the shining yellowlight. My English breakfast yoke. I so want to share with the surrounding soldiers. To be equally yoked. To pull as one and to dance as these strong shouldered boys do. With pride. With freedom. They are drumming endless humming thumbing through memory reels. Rhythm changing. Beating inside me. I let myself go. Hips moving like they knew they always could. Go. Sweat clinging to my cotton shirt. Go. Dance the dance. Let myself go.

But the dance unleashes the boys' desires. In the dark night the white eyes are flashing at me from all corners. Egg-cracked yoke smelling bad all over the desert. You can't always do what you want. I hid on the roof hoping they wouldn't come looking but they did.

Charlie Brown. The sweet Berber boy turns to demonic lust when he has too much whisky.

Charlie Brown Happy ! Everybody Happy! Charlie Brown no good drinking!

Poor big Charlie was no good with that unholy dark spirit. It drove the angel right out of him and made a warm bed for the devil inside. That demon drink.

So for the second time that summer. I was hiding away in a locked room. Madmen roaming around outside. Gazelle-like hearts racing. Beating and not beating their burning desires. The first time was down at the villa that summer with the Not so Old man. That's when the killing began. The Mistral blew the cobwebs from his not so mighty member. The all the time lurking wind blowing the spider's web from the old man's pants to release his fury. Not-so-old-man. The Villa in the summer. I can smell the Midi flowers. I can hear the sea. I can see the not so old man's dancing eyes. He wants me. That's the summer I want to talk about but I can't leap from one to another. What would we do without the spring and fall and how would we feel without the winter.

But here and now it is a Summer. I am hauled to my room. I lie still and listen to harsh guttural tongues argue. I breathe heavily sweating in the dark. A tall boy dressed in light blue and gold robes appears outside my door. He guards me right through the thick night. This calmer proud Berber boy. My hero.

In the morning the strong-shouldered bolder dancing Berberboy greets me as I walk barefoot from the wooden shower hut. Bleary-eyed desert morning.

I am sorry for my friends last night. Whisky no good. Today I take care of you.

And he held me and I knew. He is the chosen one. Lightning bolt-charged through my veins. Loves insane drain can heal the sick and maim the innocent. My desert prince making me full in this oh so empty quarter.

We walk together into the Sahara on the edge of the unknown. He touches my back with his warm black-brown skin. Berber within. He knows the way. Desire is on fire. Burning and dangerous within me. Walking up to the dunes with the Desert Prince who doesn't know his birthday and touches me with his smooth African palm. Hotbrown arm around me.

On my skin.

I stop on the dune and sit with the Desert Prince who will soon in just a few days wash my body from tip to toe like no other ever made me feel so humanly animal mineral and alive. My spirit in my head. His hands washed me all over. Soaped and stroked me. Like a dog. Scrubbed and rubbed. Cleaned my skin of it's graveyard love. Baptisma.

We talk.

Where have the Berber women gone?

You want see? I show you.

He takes me to their tent where they are sorting through dates. It is easy to find a language to communicate with these women who have chin tattoos to show their marital status. More tattoos if divorced. I have only no ring to show I am single. Not double cream-free. I give her my bracelet. All I have. She touches me and we eat dates that taste of life.

The Desert Prince and I walk barefoot into further folds of sand that are so curved I feel like I'm inside out with love. He asks if I have a boyfriend. I tell him I have had four. He is shocked but sometimes a lie is the best thing. I tell him my age.

You no say this. You no look thirty. You must not say this.

His voice is like warm hot honey drowning my senses. I ask him if he will marry one of these Berber women.

I no like not try before you buy. I like try before buy.

And later he says I meet you uncovered you stay uncovered and the biology in me remembers that I was a woman. Here with the tall smooth skinned majestic shouldered dancing boy who held a scarab and let it run over his feet. The woman in me echoed electric inside. Amazon birth Queen from the very first six. I was to leave that day but he said he would follow me. Find me. And unlike with The Pigman I wanted so much to be found.

THE PIGMAN

Now the Pigman has been a long time coming. I needed to forget him for a while. Here in the desert. He is coming. In the sun. I can see him again. Sometimes when the pink flamingos flock together in the oasis I squint at them until they become a gigantic pink pig. Then I laugh very loudly. Guffaws across the galaxies. Long before the Summer Strangulation and the Desert Cleansing and the not-so-old man in France came the Pigman. He lured us in and nearly didn't spit us out. If you need some glamour. As we all do. Here we are.

The American guy and the English gal.

In that desert there.

I lay bare my soul.

The English girl sat reading a French novel on the balcony as the sun slid down and the drink slowed down her eye.

The American guy sat writing his novel on the balcony as the sun slid down and the drink mowed down his life.

What are you reading?

Betty Blue

That's got the best sex scene in cinematic history. My name's Kuhl. Jay Kuhl. You care to join me?

I don't want to interrupt your writing.

You already did.

Tall dark and handsome. My very own Elvis from childhood idolatry. Yipee! Turns out that he is a writer just like in Betty Blue. We are in the desert as well and maybe just maybe I am going to torch his house down just like in the movie. See. Art imitating life or is it is just me. Am I imagining things?

I need a light.

And there it was.

We sitsat. Are sitting drinking. Talking. Falling into sunglassed blackhole eyes. Taxi back to his ville lair. Dogfox and vixen drinking lust and he is playing his saxophone for the first time in years as the tears roll. My kindred. My soulmate. My life so full in this oh so Empty Quarter.

I was the teacher of the rich. Arab Princes. Sheiks' children shaking their money right inyerface. Rich as the West's greed quest. I was commanded to teach the little Sheik Prince in his palace once a week. Desire is illegal in the Gulf States so you have to trap it right inside you. There is zero crime there too. It's amazing. I mean just imagine. I lived in a women's compound guarded day and night from the prowling men. Guards watch to clock the Indian peeping Tom Tom. Lusting through and at the crack. Punished slavescum Indian worker thrown back to his rathole. Space comes with wealth. Only the poor bear the stench of our shitty lives.

Beep Beep!

Hot masturbating afternoons. The chauffeur in his Merc. Pumping his horn outside my room on those hot horny afternoons and the driver sweating with desire. I drove him crazy as he drove me to little Prince Faruk's palace. Me the loyal subject. Imprisoned in the women's cells. On my way to teach sweet-smelling notsolittle balloon-faced Faruk. Chubby cheeky cheeked fleshboy with 35 cars plopped chocolates in his mouth as I tested his alpha beta betcha ain't got as much money as me.

Miss! Miss! Say for me how many cars you got.

It's not say for me it's tell me.

Yes say for me. How many, miss! How many?!

One.

And he laughed and laughed. Inbred happy. Millionaire mutant. Moneyed might. One hour later I am driven away past the women's quarters where the dry datepalm trees hang their heads in shame. Ignominious tree. Barren as the sexhole sapped of its natural flow. Driven back to my security bungalow. Locked away from dogfox men who glare and set traps to lure the vixens from their lair.

This is where I lived. Abiding their culture and taking trips into The Empty Quarter. That's what they call it on the map. If you still have the little grapefruit globe I gave you earlier. You can look and find a place called Sur. Right on the edge of Oman and if you took one of those dusty Dhow boats, made all of wood, it would sail you all the way to India. It is like the edge of the world. That's where we were. My GI Jay and I. Wooden world knocked together with wooden nails knocked into wooden shape. Withnail and I. Dhows so neatly matched to this dryold Arab painted heat. An old Dhow yard as ancient as the sea. We scrabble scramble sift through this woodsea. I find a giant wooden nail.

Is this boat wood? All made of wood?

That's right baby every damn piece.

And in the middle of this driftwood a rusty old American car. The English drifter with the rustybroken Yankee heart. Betrayed.

Betray:1 Give up treacherously (a person or thing to an enemy to punishment).

2 Be or prove false to. Be disloyal to. Disappoint the expectations of.

3 Lead astray. Deceive. Tell on. Double cross. Stab in the back. Sell down the river. Sell out. Blow the whistle on. Squeal on.

He had been betrayed by a woman. His wife. He was stuck in the Gulf war zone as she was giving head to a plumber back in the United Snakes of America. Stabbed in the back. Whistled down the squealing wind. Sold down the Savannah river. African slave lashed at the whipping post. Heart-cracked so far in two three artful parts that he would weep silent whiskytears over beers with me Mannis. A tearaway heart. Absolute beginners. The wooden dhows seduced us in the paleblue late light. The champagne sparkling wood and the russet rustbust car. East meets west and to my sun-scorched aching eyes. East was the Best.

That's where we came. My fine handsome American and me. We were lost. Adrift. At sea with not a drop to drink. Lost souls. Damned. Fallen. Irredeemable. Irreclaimable. Irretrievable. Past hope. Past praying for. Lost in the desert sandbook.

And the heat white light

Lost. In heat. Engrossed and absorbed in entranced sunblind sight. Somewhere else. Not there. Not with you. You kneel verse. Subliminal sunblindness. Atomized sublime love.

Never drive in the desert without a four-wheel drive.

So we took an estate car. Never take advise us on the edge travellers. Besides it was the last one left. Wheels are wheels.

They turn and everything changes. Is changing. Everything changed.

Whisky-driven Jay barfed and bounced across the moonscape Omani earth. Faster than we knew. Stopping here and there to stare at the light. The heat intense and dense as our love. Playing car games. Naming names. Risking it all in the name of love. Natural born thrillers. Bonnie and Clyde. Side by side. Inside each other. Tanning hides. Liberating haze of sungold nectar beer. Feeling queer steering into the lost desert time. No amber fears here when out of the jelly wobble horizonheat a rainbow family rises. Like freshwater from hell. Bedouin bodies. A mirage of optical delusion. A cacophony of colour against the painted past desert world. Jay speaks the Arabic art to dart amazement into their deep brown hot chocolate eyes.

Fin medina al Sur? Arabic.

Thirteen kilometers. Turn left. English.

You got that Mannis? says GI American Jay.

Yes I had it. Had it all the way

left…turn left…

left it somewhere on the road.

Heat dried up my brain.

Thirteen burningbright in the lightlong year kilometers later GI Jay asks.

Left or right?

And I do not know

what I left

or what I right.

So brilliant yet so elliptic.

Memory is.

We guess. We try. We stumble. We fall but we make it to The Hotel California for an Ice Cold in Alex beer. Bogart-style. A force of words that rule. Dressed to kill for dinner at the closest to the Hotel California we are gonna get in this tale.

The Pigman. The manager began his seduction with iced smiles and vodka and what a handsome couple we were and I showing more breast than I should because I was young and still didn't understand about the towers of the future and their power. Survival of the Shittest.

We so high on beer and sky. The Egyptian manager. The Pigman. A monstrous cartoon character trapped in my head. He takes us to a Dhow museum. So pleased with our crazy selves. So unaware of the plotting Pig. Pigs are pregnant for three months three weeks and three days. So acutely clever they are those pigs even though they smell of excrement. They are clean we are told. Clean. I am pure. Our Pigman now he wanted to be cleansed and remember the French guy rubbing his dick up against me in the sardine packed Gaulle de ghoultrain?

Frottage it's called. It's a French word.

Frottage definition. Rubbing. Polishing.

Se frotter, verb. To rub oneself. To provoke. Come in contact. To meddle.

I played in French once. A mad blood lusting bi-sexual Butcher screaming ....

L'eau ! les putes! On va vous frotter.

Loosely comes to us as

Water! Water! Scrub the Whores!

Frottage frothscrubbers

We don't have the same word for it in English but we English girls we loved to be fucked. Colonial cunts. All across the globe it's known that we raise hell towers. We drink. We dance and we lie open-legged to receive foreign parts. To take home from some corner of some foreign field.

That will be forever England.

So rape me please. I love it.

The drinks keep coming. We look out at the sea and feel as clean and pure as our icy vodkas which are filled again. Fleeting flashbacks. And again. Memories gift. And again. I can see the drinks placed in front of us. I reach for Jay's and The Pigman switches them back. Killerkind smile. Flashing a gold tooth that I had seen before. In Russia a long way from home. No not Russia. Kiev. In Ukraine. The Chief of Police. But we'll save that for later. I am going off course of course because Einstein blew our minds. Time is not linear so why pretend here on my whitescape beautiful page.

The drinks are drugged. Speed for Mannis. Sleep for Jay. His and hers. Ain't that nice? We talk about ourselves and our burning bright love and he is weaker. Lived longer. Hurt more and I am stronger younger and feed his hunger. We feed each other. Fat ourselves for worms. But before the worms come the pigs. Parasites. Paralytically living off the love they see. Sucking the juices out of our sprucing hearthealing. Our love drowns and rises in a vicious circle. He falters and slides as the perfect day sinks into a crestfallen moon and I help him to bed. GI Jay can hold his drink better than any man so I start to suspect something is wrong. The Pigman sees red in my too tight top. Like a red rag to a bull. He sees his little death in my big breasts. Jay mumbles about a story he wants to write about me. Showing Venus The Gulf. I help him to our room. He collapses.

JAY!

I try to wake him. Shake him but he is out. Cold. I am franticfull of energy. As jumpy as a Mexican bean and high as a ten-Tequila night and why did the English girl order the Pizza that was made to kill her?

I snatched the phone. Ravenous hunger like I had never known.

Haveyougotsomefood ?

Yes. You come to reception. Too late for deliver. You must come collect.

Collect the bingo jackpot. Come and get it. Norman Bates-style. I run to the food. Pavlov's paindriven bitch. And guess who is on the night shift? Come on down on me Pigman. Standing waiting for firstprize platter me. His angel from the sands. Splatter me. Pudgy fat faced. Fat everywhere. Clatter me. Oozing from his pants and down to his feet. Hands of sausage and lips of bacon hamstrung into the moonnight and taken in his car into the starry light. The vilevodka came too. Bile white angel spirit rotting your destined livery. I sat in the car. Eating out of his hands. Hungry horsegirl. Music loud. Head forced back.

Look at yourself.

Made to look at my eyes. In that mirror. That flips down. That some cars have.

Look! You are angel. You beautiful.

I will do anything for you. You are pure. Angelic. Beautiful. Can I touch your breasts please? This American he no love you. No deserve you. I will love you always. More than him. More than anyone. You are angel. Can I touch your breasts?

The Egyptian Pigman. Deadset on snaking inside of his Cleopatra. Head in gear. Will not be raped in this life. Will. To life. To life. To life.

Your eyes are beautiful blue. Rare. Blue. Bare breasts. Please.

Ask and you shall be given. Touching outside will not scar or jar my future love-making but inside will kill my growing honeysmile. Let be.

Touch them

and he does. Big pudgy pig paws needing kneading my breasts.

Beautiful

My mind as clearbright as the city of light. We have driven miles into the nowhere night.

DESERT DRUG RAPE ORDEAL

Ordeal: noun. Trial. Test. Tribulation. Painful/disturbing experience. Suffering. Affliction. Distress. Agony. Anguish. Torture. Torment. Calamity. Trouble. Nightmare.

And who will care and who will blame the Arab? If I get hit by a car or fucked by a dick. It's my fault. I'm not a citizen. Have no legal right to be here. If I get raped I'll… No. not. My. Path. Just took the wrong drink.

Spiked.

Feel a spike in my neck and a gleaming knife touching my nipples just enough to make them and him hard. Hard as wooden nails. Me. Close to rape. I told you. Not Jane Austen. How much closer do we want to go. Knives and hands. Love to feel these big hands on me. Mannis Poor. Come on. He stares at me like I appeared from the sky.

Marry me. I'll do anything for you. What do you want me to do?

I want to go back to the hotel.

No I want to play you a song. For you. Your name.

No! That's not my name.

It is beautiful. You are the only woman in the world.

No. I'm not a woman. Calm. I'm calm. He'll find me. GI Jay with emergency US peacekeeping forces and bombers and handsome soldiers and give us a gum chum. He'll come. He'll come with stars and stripes and the electric chair and gas and lethal injection and knock your teeth into the middle of next week. My Dad said that he'd do that. I remember. It sounded so far to be knocked. I wish him here to knock the Pigman into the middle of next year. Next Decade. Next Millennium.

Anywhere next but next to me.

The stars are twinkling winking and laughing at me.

He'll come.

No he won't. He doesn't love you. He can't come because he is weak and I made him weaker.

Spiked.

I realize as the knife traverses the line of my breast and I turn for the first time to look in Pig's eyes and say.

Can we go home now?

Missing Mannis. Mislaid. Misplaced. Misshapen. Vanished. Disappeared. Forgotten. A blank. Part of me. Gone. Forever.

Hours or seconds pass before I escape. I am escaping. Landscraping. Its hours later and he offered me all the drugs of Arabia. None of which could sweeten violated me. We smoke hashish. It calms him. As I knew it would. As I have always had perfect inner calm. Even when shook. Strangled. Knifed. No. They can't take that away from me. I manoeuvre us back to the hotel. I get my way in the end. Survival of the longest night.

The Shittest.

But as always there is magic.

The sun is rising and we could be driving home from a wonderful night for a moondance. The mountainous moonscape shimmers in near bluewhite daynight indecision. Things. As always. Are easier. In the morning. Whiteknuckle cold fear breathes well in darkness but light is coming and I am born again.

Stunning white and wholly right.

A phoenix.

Rising from the ashes of Man.

Mannis

Mannis Poor.

PARIS

Ça suffit. Enough is enough. I'm standing on the edge of Paris. Post Ireland. Post Pigman. Posted me. The périphérique freak waiting with leather bags leather jacket and black leather heart. Waiting for the man. The fix it man. The rich South of France man. The Not-so-old man. The French man who is Swiss/Irish//Danish/Scottish/English yet looks like The President of the United States of kiss my arse. The fix it man has come to collect me from the side of the road and other men in lorries shout things in French.

Tu s'est fait jetée par ton mari?

Have I been thrown out by my husband. I smile. That word, it makes me smile. I am a new Parisian with a clean slate here to build bridges and standing on one. Waiting. Searching for a room of my own. Leaving behind kind Madame Polle who told stories of her North African travels and missed her dead and buried husband who also looked kind and I have as good ole Tenneesee phrasecoined so often relied on the kindness of strangers. Her house crowded with artefacts from her pied noir life. And a huge balance scale hanging over my head at dinner. Foreign. Over here. Over sexed and underpaid. God bless the American church off The Elysian Fields. The small blue notice a scrap of papermagic carpet that flies you direct to paradise.

Ad. 8 arr. Une studette 15mètres carrés.

immeuble mezzanine 0615870696

I phone the number and the Not So Old Man answers.

Bonjour

Ma voix

my voice

My mother fell in love with my father's voice. I am my father's daughter. Lightning bolts through his clogged arteries, veins swell, untravelled routes open as his tinman heart blushes king crimson. He will remember this time again and again. The time he heard my voice. His life begun again. He rattled around his villa with fullforce vigour and falling so hard in love when the serotonin in your brain shoots up skyhigh and then plummets to the lowest point. And remember love can cure the sick and maim the innocent.

Je téléphone à propos…le la l'appartement dans l'église Americaine….

Do you want to speak English?

His voice a rich patriarch of oldtimes when women listened and men told. Where women sewed and wrote secretly for fear of death by drowning witchstyle or leached for hysteria. Thank the Lord for more modern times. Frances Farmer locked away in an asylum wishing there really was a morning but at least she got a room of her own. The good old days where women's feet were bleeding in too tight shoes and corsets squeezed their breath. A voice that would catch the fainting lady. A chivalry that is not dead. Those were the days my friend when a man knew where he was and an uncle could have his way fingering the daysoftheweek knickers touching the young ones lives and pushing his mighty member in and out. Monday In and …Tuesday…out…The blood begins to flow down into his pants. His not-so-old pants skipping his brain and hatching this child-like colossus back into the sexual world. Bring back the good old days. Pumping pumping blood for money. Blood money Judas-style. Why thank you I've often relied on the kindness of bloodsucking strangers.

It's a small studette. Ideal for a single young lady like yourself. Oh you're an English teacher! How wonderful! My father he loved England. You can come and see it on Monday.

The not so old man puts down the portable piece that has just plugged him back into life. He looks out at the sea in his Southern Midi paradise and thinks of me. Sunshine tingles to his bones. He must return to Paris tout de suite. This voice surely is the call of an angel. The mountains meet the sea. All things in law divine. In one spirit meet and mingle why not I with thine? He knows he can buy anything he wants.

I have always got what I wanted. I have never been rejected in my life.

You can't always get what you want.

In the meantime. So mean is time. We see Mannis tip tapping down Avenue Posh like a Dickensian matchgirl drinking in the succulent sights of unashamedly slick richy rich wealth and stealth. The artful dodger escapee from South London scumsville any mug foots the bill for a baresquare inch of nothingness in the peesmelling dwellings of Blewisham Batterclapperseaham and the streets are paved with gold only you have to have your head stoned to see it. This pavement gold. Kicked and bashed on the street by bully boy wot wot nigger screamers heading their BNP quarters in the leafy suburbs of joy. Net curtain twitching bitching about the refugee sea-swell from the incontinent continent. Here the BNP is a bank in a swank quartier. So artful this dodging as I skipscrape down my avenue of gold where the newest nannies smell of Swedish sweat as they fold the petit bourgeois clean white daysoftheweek knickers listening to Piaf and dreaming of romance after dark. And I. Mannis Poor head for number one with the biggest door I have ever seen. In a dream. I step over the threshold and smile. Most people have never had more than two thousand pounds at one time and who wants to be a millionaire. I don't. I don't. I really don't.

Greedily greeted by the Madame de Châteaux Papa has eneuf is enough. I come with police escort flanked by my very own protection courtesy of a friend's man. The madame is impressed and confused by my gendarmerie who think the place is small and poky and not fit for a lady like me. Madame de gold-rolled earrings complete with vicious Japanese tittle-little pooch is the femme of the rollicking-richman right now on the bullet-through-the-heart train back from the south.

La femme. Definition: woman and wife but no wife was this trouble and strife. No coarse divorce as catholic guilt spilt she does not want to lose the château in Normandy and the title gained from the brute who beat her black and blue. She would turn any colour if it ends in gold. Come on down if the price is right and humiliate wildly the greedyguts humanrace who can't keep up the pace of money money money that flimsy weapon of self-destruction. A lady in distress saved and undressed by her live in not-so-old loverman. A femme afraid of wrinkling tinkling age caging her female womb-tomb. Dreaded drying up of the wet dream. She is taut. Tightly smiling. Seeming but not true. Much to the handsome gendarmerie's chagrin I accept Madam's offer of this dingy studette. Then out of the blue a call from the not-so-old man and an offer to help me move. Sunday. Dimanche. Midday. It's no problem really Mannis as he manoeuvres a lone journey without the Madame of control. I'll pick you up. I'll fill you up. You need never worry about anything again. Full fridges no more mouldy green on your insides as outside the sun slides into the courtyard.

So like I said I stand like a périphérique freak waiting for the fix it man…

Tu s'est fait jetée par ton mari?

The pink flamingos drink from the oasis in my desert evening's eye. Staring at the water I see the reflection of purples and pinkish waterlily light. Visions fastforward me to a summer day of kite-soaring joy.

I remember. Yes!

Monet's garden.

A MEMORY OF MONET LOVE

I wish I could remember some things. Like the girl with the red curly hair. Her name. I remember how cool she was. And I think if I saw her now I would have to speak although she never spoke that much. She could draw you see. Good with her hands.

In Love.

Once upon a time we went to Monet's garden. It is so full of lilies and light and we. You and me admiring his spiralling force to creature create such flowers on a plate with teasing tree light and you my love with red locks of curl. I. Your golden girl. We sit and drip into each other as the sun melts the creamy Camembert. Can we bear the beauty? You use black and white photopresent polaroid to capture the light.

Click .

I have a photo of us. The light is so bright that it is difficult to tell the difference between the flowers and us. You and I there in black and white. You hide from the technicolour world so vast it be so unfurled. Trick of memory lane light that Monet got so right and the feelfine wine makes us feel sublime and happiness is not a crime as we walk Huck Finn style back through the fields sharing the bottle that gives us the courage to love again.

Singing Monet Monet Monet in a rich man's swill. We find ourselves on a bank lying heads in laplove of comfort in one another's company under the willow tree dreaming of Ophelia drowning with her daisies and long purples that liberal shepherds give a grosser name.

She and I.

Gemini twinned.

Right.

But some maids give them a grosser name. I can feel it coming closer. Dead men's fingers. The human finger tastes like porksausage and in exchange for what would we eat our fellow human beings. Feeding cow to cow ends in tears and I see the future as the pigs are hung upside down burning in their thousands. I see the not-so-old man's fingers floating in the sea. Lying in Monet's sunlight I smile at my love.

Barbecued brown me.

Strawhaired and who can make hay of this bale?

And if I was a flower I would be a Rose.

A desert rose.

Crystallised by time.

Here in my sandscape.

MEETING THE NOT-SO-OLD-MAN

Mild headpains from drinking as I stand waiting. My innards twisted and sick of love. The not-so-old man on a promise to help me as soon as he heard my voice as he sipped his rosè in his dream house in the south. He knew I was the one he had been waiting all his sixty-eight not-so-many years for. I who walked with a purpose he had never witnessed before. Striding me across the grand courtyard through the gates of heaven. I have come to delight his tongue like the sea salt oysters he devoured. I. The final pièce de résistance in his moveable feast.

In the African desert clusters of super-novas and constellations feel biblical. The Northern star shining brighter than the others. Peopled stars stand-alone like the Pole Star or form clusters. Groups. Families. The dogs are howling and the call to prayer is reassuring in some ways as I sleep like a baby. Breathing better and my white kaftan feels pure against my golden brown body. A miracle of life this purging and renewal.

He will find me.

He will wash me clean again.

She is standing on the side of the road and I am weak at my knees to see this English beauty. Mannis. My Mannis. We will be soul-mates. Lovers. I kiss her hello and something in her eyes is calling me to my father who loved the English.

My Daddy. Dagda. Daddy.

My Ariel has come just when I was ready to die.

The tap on the shoulder the insistent time dripping

tap tap tap

and on turning I find not death but

LOVE.

Poetry…Blake…Shelley..

The view in Serenity like a mantra for you my golden girl

The fountains mingle with the river
And the rivers with the Ocean
The winds of heaven mix for ever
With a sweet emotion
Nothing in the world is single
All things by law divine
In one spirit meet and mingle
Why not I with thine?

My heart is slowing down but now I see her. I can breath again. Pumping blood to my weakening heart. Thank you Mannis for making a not so old man very happy. Hop skip and a jump. I will. I will find the will to life.

The will to live.

I Can.

CAN! CAN!

Cancan: a lively dance of French origin orig. a form of quadrille now performed by a woman and involving high kicks usually while holding up the front of the skirts.

Duck Mannis! dive into the warm Mediterranean Sea. Kick up your legs. Monroe-creaming heat warming the cockle of his heart. Inside out in the street for all to see. Wearing you inside out.

Wear: Exhibit. Present a facial expression. Appearance

Wear out :

1 Impair the surface of or obliterate gradually by friction. Use.

Attrition.

2 sap the strength of. tire. fatigue. exhaust. overcome by persistence.

See the mountains kiss high Heaven
And the waves clasp one another;
No sister flower would be forgiven
If it disdained its brother
And the sunlight clasps the earth;
And the moonbeams kiss the sea
What is all this sweet work worth
If thou kiss not me?

Who knows what goes on behind a face. In someone else's headtime? He was a kind man helping me move. Streetwise naïve me.

He sees his greatest love and I see a paternal friend. Helping me find a home. Wearing my red boots for luck. Click them. I will be there but it's too soon to leave the yellow brick road. I am getting closer to the desert. Closer to the light. My very own Wizard of Oz where alchemy will alter the ache.

He takes my baggage and we drive through Paris. The city makes you as high as the Eiffel tower in the glass lift that shoots you up to the top. Lucky to be here.

Remembering other journeys.

The long train from Prague to Russia.

Reading Dostoeyevski. Sitting. Legs dangling from the back carriage. Railway children style. Daddy my Daddy! Offered fish and champagne and a hard bed for five dollars and a night with a Russian soldier who I gave myself too to thank him for all those lives lost to the moustachioed devil sperm. Lives lost in some corner of some foreign field. In the Ukraine I see the gold leafed palaces of this sufficient pageant and I see the Chief of Police's gold teeth knocking back the vodka. Instructed to copy him. It's only polite. I do the same. One sip of gruel to one shot of vodka. Sip. Shot. Sip. Shot. Slurp. Shot. And then a search for beer in the bone-dry bar domed city. Ugly grey blocks saved by blasts of gold leafed beauty lifting you up out of the mire. Clarity fire. Like each vodka shot interspersed with a soapy soup. A trip to see the police station and this is where we work and here is my colleagues and here is my office and here is my foul-smelling breath and just a kiss for Mr. Policeman who takes care of you little girl and here is my iron rod of steel pressed inside you and just one …I slip out like a butterfly glimpsed only once maybe twice but rarely a third time *filer à l'anglaise*. I quickly nifty duck and dive from my biology but it will catch me one day. It will come.

And outside the rain but no pain as there in Kiev a wonderful small man followed me everywhere with his umbrella.

In fact I don't mind the .rain.

You will if it kills you and he smiled. The fall-out nuclear style from Chernobyl a world away from my mind. I keep my head up. I look at the gold leafed palaces as acid rain falls.

From Russia with Love.

We reach Etoile.

Etoile. The Star points shining out from those deadunknown men. Fate astral action spinning me into newness. Catherine wheeling over the sea rocks and desert flamingo flocks. I understand why Beckett wanted to move here. The city whirls you into happiness.

Decadence walking every inch of its pigeon grey paths. Here I am nearer the world. Nearer the desert but not yet. I've had a bellyful of this ignorance more than a bellyful said my Chekhovian servant back in Ireland as we were leaving our childhood home.

Vive! La France!

We say clown faced and cherries painted on my neck as the blows hit my orchard.

Memorydrive.

We drive through the Irish night to find a drinking hole. I shaking from the emotion of the last performance. The car shaking from the tempest torn night. Wind. Rain. And Sam swerves as he nearly hits a fallen tree. Fallen Angel. Me. A tree lying sapscreaming across the windrain battered road. A Collatin Oak plundered by the British to build our parliament. Democracy from the wooden hearts of others. More than a bellyful.

The secret admirer spins around the Arc de Triomphe and I love the lack of order as cars nearly collide and we swing into my new street. Number 1. That's me. Avenue Hoche. Don't pronounce the H and don't talk to me about destiny.

MY PARISIAN PRISON

Here. J'arrive. A studette on Avenue Hoche off the Etoile Arc de Joyful and Triumphant. Right on my doorstep. The world at my feast in my exclusive quartier with my very own guards for protection thanks to my neighbours at the Saudi Arabian Embassy. 24 hour guards who surely know how to protect a lady. Now ain't this posh full of ladies weighed down by gold and lightening the load with small yapping dressed up mutton as lamb damn poodle-terrier-bury-her bourgeois dogs. Dogs of war enjoying the booty of colonialism. Dressed to impress these perfumed canines. Tiny tempers spreading the city with well-placed shit. Strolling in the park with its follies and dolly families and café au lait and I love it. Seize the decaying day. The studette so très très français-the bedsit we torturers English call it. So hard we are. So barely violent and sexually scared as we sit pale and shivering in masturbation degradations in our isolated bedsits. I prefer studette. We enter the grand courtyard with a door inverted-Alice style towering over my head. Like Madame Polles' balance. Oh to be foreign and I'm full of the cabin-like home that is only for me with its wooden beams and mezzanine. A word I never knew and now I'm living in one. Studette with a mezzanine. Sounds like raspberries and cream to me.

Step ladder bunk-bed memories of me and my brother and the worlds we created at the bottom of our beds. We both wanted Mrs. Wright at our bottom of bed towns because she was warm and wise and old. Soothsaying-smooth lines lapping at the edge of her owly eyes and secure like a night home with an open fire and a book that takes you so far inside it that you never wanna step out. I guess we would never have had any Stranglers or Pigmen down there. No. We would've had a sign up saying No Stranglers or Pigmen if we'd known about them then.

No pain in here. Except my gin kicked soaked lostlove broke childlike nope no. NO! I want it. Can't have it twists and turns. Just me and the not-so old man who shows me around this wooden ship cabin of fifteen mètres carrés. They love that the French everything measured in square metres. The schoolpaper. All squares. I love the French. They are so damn funny. So proud of themselves yet really shy at the same time. Anyways they are so hated by Les Anglo Saxon that I tip the balance some days. Screaming Vivre La France! at any opportunity and 'allez les bleus !' when they win the football and knock out that oh-so-bright I'm bloody-so-right wing Britgit. Waving my Red Cross. Fighting the firedragon. They who knock the little girl off her Daddy's shoulders on the terror terraces of years gone by. Those were the days my friend. They who freedom was fought for. They who win wars in bloodthirsty colour red whitefear and numbblue tears. Dead bluebody fears. They who sing songs whilst bashing up Belgian bars coz *IT LOOKS BETTER LIKE THAT* and Chelsea smiles and *YOU KNOW WHAT THE PROBLEM WITH FRANCE IS?*

No please tell me.

It's full of fucking French people.

Bemused galled Gauls look on horrified. I try to explain exactly what a Chelsea smile is and why the football yob ringleader who slashed the gnashers bloodred got ten years inside. Rule Brittania! Brittania Rules the waves! Britain never never never shall be slaves. Slavs or ghoulish garlic sodden Gauls.

Lord deliver us from evil and strangle the right people.

I later tell Mr Kim. My private student. A Korean businessman with spy fantasies. I tell him I like my studette. I like it its very Parisian.

Yes like a prison!

He is shocked by my seemingly shabby dark Jack the Ripper red abode.

No! Parisian. It's got character.

From where on he always referred to it as my 'character place' in that light Oriental sing-song sound that makes everything sound like a take-away.

So the not so old man shows me my room. The television is on top of the microwave which is on top of the fridge and on Sunday nights if you can't sleep there is a Porn channel ohh nothing too hard you know just to help you sleep. Us English girls you see raising flesh towers all over. In his dancing eyes. I didn't yet know that he had fallen in love with the first shot of the film. Me. Mannis in leather by the side of the road. A lady of a sort in distress. Left him reeling and we the innocent are just living.

ARTICHOKE HEART

The heart definition 13: the dense inner wood of a tree hardened by age and lacking functional vascular tissue.

The not-so-old man's heart was not notsoold. It had taken a bashing in wars. Seen hanging women tortured by the Ayatollah. Met Charles de Gaulle and laughed heartily. Smoked Woodbines and Embassy. Dished out fatalfags to the pygmies. Loved Lincoln England with the secret imps and lived long and hard in the Iranian desert. And now giving his loved one Iranian stone jewels made the old heart pump again. The medicine men can do wonders to make that pump keep pumping but love says the notsoold man love is the cure and so here is my lady of the lamp.

My soulmate that I never found through the years of the bourgeois bores and the bragging bridge nights and the pumped up powdered saggies who will not pump this strong man's heart. But Mannis is here with her smile and her eyes and laugh and love of art and poetry and I have fallen in love.

Letters. The man starts to write letters in an attempt to gradual woo me. The French lessons in the dimly lit studette that left me adrift. Complicated grammar once deciphered showed all he wanted was all of me. An invitation to dine. Excused by a dying father of the Madame de Control. My landlady and his girlfriend of 18 years Ann-Marie who just may not be here this weekend. We could drive in the country. How I loved the drive with you Mannis even though you were sick I was so close to you. I could feel you. Anything need fixing. Doing? Any hole need filling? Mannis there is a hole in you. You have never loved have you?

A fairy plum plucked right off the eau de vie Christmas tree. Sugar Daddy. Feed her sugar Daddy. She'll be yours. Returning to stocked fridges magically bursting with goodies of salmon fresh and champagne to blow the bubbles into her and be sure that her balloon world never bursts. Snapped into Mary Poppins order and me Mannis begun to realize as I had always known that Santa does exist and all he wants is my happiness.

Landlord increasingly homing in on me. The old goat riding red on my rat-ta-tat door wanting chunks of me. Sucking my goodness. Kissing me craftily and hard on the lips like your grandad when you are small. Takes the thrill of pushing his hand that little tittle too far up the tartaned itchy dress. I do not turn my cheek in time. I feel I have entered into incestuous games with the not so old man. I hear prostitutes don't kiss on the lips so why should I?

Perhaps you would fancy a tour of the markets and we could have some oysters.

Those creamy fleshy white juicy tasting lips of your clever crevice and cute cunt.

Telegram reads: Sensing danger. Caught in a trap
The parasites will come warned GI Jay. Oh where u now? Drugged
by the United Snakes of Amnesia. The lascivious insidious man
draws on her smile.

Come for lunch Ann-Marie is away!

Her father is dying and I cannot comprehend this loss. It whitebare bulb terrifies me to think of it. If my lover was wooing another as my father was dying. It stinks. Do unto others as you would never have done to yourself. I mount the stairs. He says 'climb'. He has elegant English. A real gent sits me down and pours me a Scottish malt a man 'after my own heart', definition 14: just such as one likes or desires.

So marvellously gloriously achingly Paris with oysters shrimps and crisp crystal wines and leafy courtyard sunslant nearwild heaven. I am opulent decadent alive as the juicy fleshy oystercunt slips inside me. I think of silk slits and big Daddies towers of pleasure. I have a special feeling for you Mannis. He invites me to his villa in the summer. The summer. Shows me photos of something heaven is made of and I feel the cream in my insides sliding out and into him as he makes love to my eyes with his tales of Iranian deserts and a mysterious cat that howls and wails into the desert night.

A lunch with an oil Baron. A fairy rich slick guy to stop my wallet creaking. Wine and dine me at the Maison de Caviar drunk on balls of popping black babies. The delight of the oral salty abortion. The water in us. In the caviar. The oyster the saliva and here in the desert the water is life. Thirst quench me as the sun reaches higher and my body grows warmer. Water of life flood through me. Desert Prince wash me throughout.

Inside and out.

Inside and out.

In and out.

Skin on skin memories brushed back to life. I use dye from blackberries mixed with clay browns-his soul soars as I smear the walls with creamy brown-cinnamon spices. This Hindu man gave me good loving on my memory skinflesh.

The Parisian streets are wet and it's fiercely cold. Waiting to see the genius Brook play in the insalubrious district of Barbes. Barbes-a short tube blast from The Champagne Fields but a whole world away...African dresses, flipflops, flea markets- puces, and Tati..oh Tati where you can buy all the tat you fancy....The Moroccan cafes are full of horny men, alley cats on heat, and lost solitary women. Western women intent on objectifying their desires- us wicked women as they have learnt are easy, open for business 24/7, no strings attached, no hidden catch just free love. The cheap scent of freedom. A small price to show your face and feel your hair blow in the wind and glow in the sunshine. I order a glass of wine and the waiter asks me where I am from.

London.

Oh! I love London.

The other men stand at the bar staring. I smoke a cigarette, polish off my wine and leave. Here in Paris there are small, circular tables for one-solitary diner, fine except if you are a woman alone when the crowds have blown. Men fear women will laugh at them. Women fear men will kill them. Well ain't that just dandy. On the street corner of Barbes the theatre building looks shabby and run-down as any true theatre for the people should. There is a power cut so no food is being served before the show. I have the hunger. I wander through the damp streets lashing Parisian rain, sullen wintercold Parisian faces, blank smudges heading for the homescape. Inside a window I see rows of dark-skinned men wolfing down Indian food. Steamy windows. No frills. Canteen style. I enter and squeeze into the only vacant space on the bench. White woman standing out like a sore thumb, flushed pink raspberry amidst nutmeg, cocoa smooth faces glowing from the spicy hot food. Unlike the French bar no one cares I'm here-they are happy in their skin-*bien dans sa peau.* Except one man opposite me. He is eating with his hand, his skin is deep walnut, smooth as mahogany melted chocolate. Handsome chiseled features fit for Bollywood.

Are you British?

Yes.

I love the British.

He places his hand on his heart and then opens it to me like the Berbers do.

I hate the French-they are cunning like foxes.

I laugh and for the next 20 minutes I am in stitches. His smile is infectious. He talks animatedly of yoga, the Kama Sutra and Bollywood.

The Indians can't live without Bollywood.

The other men's eyes are glued to the TV above our heads.

Look at them, they don't even blink- their eyes are stuck.

We laugh, snigger and giggle.

I studied the Karma Sutra for two years. I am a very good teacher. I make massage with Ayevedic oils-it like magic.

I give you massage

I'd love that. I have been teaching stressed out French businessmen to speak English. Not an easy task! Boof!

I will give you pleasure.

Ok but I have to go to the theatre now. Will you wait for me?

Yes of course buddy

During Adrien Leister's Hamlet I keep seeing his face-shining dazzling smile. After the Queen is poisoned and Hamlet dead -he is waiting for me underneath the pigeon -grey pont. We take the metro to my room in Passy. Paris is a numbers game and the 16th is the jackpot arrondissment for pleasant, monied Parisienne perfection-oozing cheese and strong coffee delights for the ageing wealthy bourgeoisie who hold the key to such luxuries. Shades of Last Tango in Paris filter my mind as we hurry along Birtakim in Brando's footsteps-images of Maria Schneider naked in the bath, washed down by Marlon and of course the butter scene…Madhu stops me suddenly and we kiss on the tiny bridge, winter cold thawing now as he presses his body close to mine. He is like an excited teenager, puppy in heat overwhelmed with fervour-I fancy that.

In the apartment my Bardot landlady has left a note- *N'hésitez pas!*

There is beer and champagne in the fridge. We open two beers. Sip.

Ready?

I enter my room, all dimly lit in Parisian reds, the enormous bed takes up the whole room-a true boudoir.

He undresses me and I lie face down not knowing what to expect. Thrilled with anticipation. His hands, warm and loving begin to caress my back-the oils smell sweet, as he rubs and caresses my skin his breathing quickens, becoming faster and deeper. His hands explore reaching deep into me finding the spaces and places that make me flinch. When he reaches my feet his fingers go up and around my toes bringing me shuddering ecstatic pleasure. His fingers reach up and stroke me gently at first, then inside, slowly out, and in and up and around. I am moaning and jumping like a wildcat.

I think you like it.

He is really hard now, excited as a young boy when he first feels his hard flesh rise and blood pump. He maneuvers himself on top and starts to rub up and down. I can feel his hard cock tip threatening to enter me. He pushes the tip in just slightly- the sense that all is to come, building pulsating through me. My body convulses as he cleverly pushes inside me and then denies me until I am weeping and crying in my need to be filled up-made whole. Finally, he gives me his whole self. Total fusion. I contract my muscles feeling electric as this December night splices my soul. My little death.

Now I need something raw and animal-barebody stone-aged strong. I turn around and lift my arse towards him-he responds and pushes his cock up inside me. The rhythm rocks. I turn again and push him as far as I can get-we both lock hands as waves of orgasm rush us. Man and Woman at their best. Together.

Thank you India.

He tells me he is a dancer and moves his head from side to side. His dark steel head lays on my soft breast as he licks and sucks.

We switch on the radio and dance naked to French rock ballads-he is hard again and enters me during the dance-my breasts feel good against his chest as I start to convulse in short bursts. He is much bigger inside me this time-how men grow with passion and confidence. Chemistry is no coincidence as some people crack and burn while others fizzle out-damp squibs stuck in the mud. He leads me to the bed and withdraws just before he releases his deadly cargo onto my chest. To be or not to be-that split-second question. Penetrations penance interrupted. No ancient patter dawn.

Just for this moment. I feel the world is good and kind. I ask him to leave as I cannot sleep with a stranger-it is far too intimate. He understands and says we will always be great friends. As I fall asleep I dream of India-The Taj Mahal and Maharajah, cows roaming free, bright Hindu gods with blue breasts, young horny boys waiting on dusty train tracks with rampant desires and the fat old pumpkin sun going down on a Goan beach.

THE FALL

It is autumn now and then in Paris. I picked up a conker that day as big as a tangerine with the shape of a baby's bottom. It made me feel happy to sit with that conker in my hand. Smooth and brown and autumn. When I was a child I loved to play conkers. I was good. I was a tomboy. King of the marbles conkers bonkers piano-scratching bundled up sack-of-potatoes belted up sent to school with yellow socks and bovver boots on classphoto day hero. Never the bows in the hair-square elastic skipping nit-picking Barbie collecting girl. I kicked the conker. Vinegar soaked. I footballed hard. My Dad. I love him. He went up the school in a 'let the kid play for the team she is better than half the boys' bid but no. Not then. I was an acorn-throwing glasshouse smashing chopper-riding devils-dropping over the handlebars finger hanging off feel no fear tough cows-lick kid.

I walk in the walking city of light to Musée Rodin and get some good stone vibes. Good God. What a gorgeous garden full of sculptures that are so heavy yet look so light. The lightness. I have. I love. They hit you immediately and the day is perfect. Leaves and crisp air and singing birds. The usual but not usual. Think.

The leaves. The crisp air. The singing birds.

I bet we both had this at the bottom of our beds. He does hands well this Rodin. So well. Feel the enormity of a man's hands. The power and love of large hands makes my small hands feel tiny and I think of my father's hands. My mother's soft Oil of Ulay kind hands. A lover's musical piano hands that played me till I sang to a tune so high so perfect that it has only since become a scream. Hands inside and out. Out before in is good and inside out. In out.

In out…

So we are beginning and ending in the summer and here is the autumn after the summer from which we begun with the strangulation and the not-so-old man is hanging on for spring when he can be king and captain of the yacht. I'm the captain right or wrong goddammit and this heart will pump. Will beat. Will not beat me – will flow.

And then a blow.

His best friend in the whole wide grapefruit world dies.

2000

Winter rain came and went and Jesus died 2000 years ago. The first hint of sunshine sublime rises from the grimgray bonecold ashes. Normandy for a landing of Poor proportions. All descending on a château for my beau frère's 50th. It was a surprise for him. A wonderful surprise. I arrived with a Frenchman in tow. Vegetarian immovably opinionated fish out of water at an Anglo-Saxon family feast from the land of the seafaring booze cruisers. Binge-drinking connoisseurs of wine-tasting in Calais car parks. My Dad thought Stephan was on drugs and my Oil of Ulay Mum just worries am I happy as he shies away from the loud crowd Poors and will not dance to the mad Nordic rhythms of us Supertroupers. Dancing Queens. Drunkenly celebrating our own Waterloos.

Wonderful château with my brother and his new baby. So now he really has something special at the bottom of his bed and I love them all as we rollick and play posh in this bastion of secret family love. It reminds me of The Cherry Orchard house in Ireland where we performed and lit the whole place with candles and The Strangler took a front row seat and I held my neck as I. From the gutter but looking at the stars uttered utter irony.

I feel something like the hand of death on me

and the house was hot that night.

My childhood my innocent childhood

Magic to be with my family playing table tennis and cards as though the years had slipped away and Elvis had just died. The crushing blowstrike of my first death and my brother broke the news as I stood trying to keep warm in our tiny condensation dripping bedroom. I was 7. In the South they say *When Elvis died it was like losing a brother.* I know what they mean. My sisters wore black for days so he has always been like God for me. We wrote his name in round playing cards with Union Jacks on the back in the Cornish wetsandy beaches and every day I woke to Nothing quite as pretty as Mary in the morning and to this day here his voice does things to me that no-one can take away.

Lovely nieces running around and so glad to have this extending family and not a newly coined let's pretend two people breaking up doesn't split the kids heart clean in two because as Aimee Mann says One is the loneliest number that you'll ever do. New world Americanas feelgood P.C plodding language. Not single parent family. We are binuclear. I always hated nuclear war. My Mum always said it would be OK and she's been right up till now. I love her for that. If they were giving out an award for making you feel better. Reassurance in times of dire global fears. My Mum would win hands down.

Hands up who wants to hold the baby?

The icing on the beau frère's cake. This golden nephew boy with the face of a cherub. Bending down to say goodbye as all the family sit on the steps for photos and something breaks inside. Tears flow as my Mum and Dad showdrive us to the station.

The sky hurt me a lot when I looked at it and the umbilical ripping tearing feartears. The sky. Blue and deep red felt like a deep bruise inside and out. Like death and endings. Later I learnt that the not so old man had been pulling on my strengths to get him through his best friend's funeral.

That night I tried to shut the world out tying a scarf ten times tight round my eyes. Stephan tried to prise me open. Pull my blindfold away to face the nightday. To reach inside. To show me the light but the black dog was breathing down my neck with all its might. Dragging me down. Stealing my clown. He was there staring hard. On the seat with me. A lump of lard.

The train finally pulled into Gare de Lyon. I stepped out onto the grey platform. Concrete welcome.

Paris felt cold and war-like that night.

Silence. I stare. The shameless sheltering desert sky is reassuring and constant like the present. No shifting tectonic bruise plates as seen in the icy north Viking lands. In the African desert on the edge of the Sahara near the Algerian border. An outpost truly in the middle of nowhere. Dune robbed me. Robbed sobbed. Wiped out. Erased. Effaced. Extinguished identity. Personality carefully delicately built up blotted out in a blast. Covered with nature's sandhand. There is only outside here and I can see my inside as clearly as the dunemoon that towers above me. Me a blot on the landscape.

Spring soon.

THE BUTCHER OF NICE

In Paris I fall in with a crowd of actors. The International troupe de Bohemian and passionate. The director asked me to play a butcher. A lesbian butcher covered in blood who shouts alot. We rehearse for long days in Paris until we drive through the night to Nice to tell our playstory. The screaming mad butcher blood-lusting role fills my soul with a great release of red-rage. The Vache folle and I. The Mad English Cow. Strangled. Mauled. And always ASKING for it. La viande! Chez camarade! The play is Russian. Suicidé in French. The suicider. Everyone wants the main man Simon to kill himself for one reason or another. For Communism for The Church or for Sex. I want him to die for the meat. La Viande! I am a butcher of hearts. I take them out and eat them.

Walking through the dunes with no audience walking backwards through EinSteintime dimensions. Walking on stage in Nice.

Eh bien voilà...personne!

And well there we are. Nobody. There is nobody here. Bare naked actor look them in the face and show the space. The faster you go the smaller things look in your blackhole soul. I walk on stage. I step out of my cage. I walk down the steps. The Mistral is blowing. It's the summer. I walk into the trap laid so sweet bonbon naïve. Come here little girl. Come and get the goodies. Be a baddie Daddyo. I am running down the cliff. I see him walking into the sea. The not so old man. Brave ancient old man of the sea. Heading for a watery grave Opheliastyle but Hamlet is a girl and to be or not to be hung from a tree is the question. His gray hair glints ghostly in the Mediterranean night. Mistral palm leaves. I am walking. My toes touch the grains of sand so finely blown into glass. The glass smashes. He cannot breath in his Masterbuilt house swimming in rosé. The wind. The sea. The dolphin and then maybe it's time for the summer.

THE MAN WHO HAS EVERYTHING

You are dolphin you are like me.

One summer leads to another back and forth in hotwarm nights here in my desert soulhole. I sit horizon gazing as The Desert Prince massages my back back to life and as his hard African palms pull and press my skin. I remember oozing Ouzo days of carefree camping inside nature. A friend in need of Salvation and there I was the Army to rescue her from the addicted lover.

A friend. Companion. Crony. Mate. Bosom friend. Comrade. Playmate. Soulmate. Intimates. Confidante. Familiar. Pal. Chum. China.

My old china platemate was so fragile then. Teetering on the edge of the old Greek wooden display cabinet. Thin and smokescared as a rabbit darting away from the lights. Her big brown eyes sunk deep in care for her Bigbear who was lost in Naked Lunch despair. Blown skyhigh Burroughs burrowed down inside his junksunk self and poor old Leila was on her knees digging in the well but could not lift him out. Scrabbling and scratching until her nails were chipped and charred.

SOS Save our souls

Save. Rescue. Free. Set free. Liberate. Deliver. Snatch. Bail out. Salvage. Redeem.To save from sinful desires. Protect. Safeguard. Keep. Shield. Screen. Preserve. Conserve.

Save someone's soul save our own.

A friend in need is a friend in deed. Action speaks louder than words. I know I have not spoken for sometime. Heartsbroken.

A friend? Have you got one? Invisible or real? Some say they are but only you know the real ones. The ones who bail you out of the pail in sickness and in health. Stealthy wealth of love without the white-wig edge sly-judge phoney sludge falsefriends have. Whispering out of the corner of mouths. Backstabbing side-walking crabs. Fair-weather death slabs.

My friend's lived too long with the Heroin Man. Heroinshots through his veins so he could stay deep inside and never need to come out. Cottonwool numb. So comfortable this little Greek macho.

Love rescue me.

We.

My very best friend and I.

We took ourselves to the sea and a tent makes three. And my dear friend hanging food in the trees as though the bears were coming. Lying on the ground. Rough and stony. We listened for snakes but you can't always hear them can you? Hissing us into the holiday of fantasies and octopus hanging over our heads as we drank retching Retsina. Bittersweet in its clarity.

Ouzo white light of grabbing Greece. A feast of simplicity in blue and white. A race to the sea with an animalman who bit and scratched like the dog he was. So alive he was. The man who had everything. I remember walking through the fisherofwomen village with two old craggy fishermen who saw us caught in their nets. My very best friend. She decides she would like to marry a fisherman. Fish everyday. Fishing for something pure and simple. Not wild-haired white eyeball popping fagbutt fireball beddanger at night with the heroinhead lover. I want to show her love inside out. We visit the monasteries towering in the sky. Meteora high. Winching the wenches up to the tower in search of salvation. The Nunnery with candles in whisky bottles where they lend you a skirt to cover your sinfulskin. Thou shalt not Kill. Thou shalt not.

The two old fishers of women took us in their boat and wanted their wicked way but we did not play. We were only there for the ride and on return from the chugging boatjourney we walk into town Waynewestern style. Hands at hips. Beauties and their beasts. We the beauties go to buy the blacklung sticks from the kiosk man who is animal man.

You come with me you are dolphin like me. You come my farm. I have all.

The tall gentle German friend followed on his Harley and the animal man was virility in flesh. Strong. Wired. Alive. He drove us speed of light fast. So fast and my outside began to shrink and my insides grew and grew and grew.

Leila left with the gentle kind German. A man good with bones. A Physiotherapist feeling her battered heroinspoilt skeletonskin and bones back to life. Neglected untouched skin cannot win without the Midas love touch. Shrivels and dies without the love guise. Stroke your bedkin before you turn hell hound turn away.

There are good men Leila. I promise.

But I want the animalman. I can hear his blood pumping through his veins. The woods burnished bright bracken of drought delight. I am walking up the beach and he wants a race. A human race. Man. Woman. Man and Girl. Girl and Boy. One and two and three waiting in the sea.

You run. You are fast. You are dolpin. You are like me.

And I am like him. Girled by Man. Hurled by earthbound speed to seaspirit saltwashing glory. V for Victory! We race to the sea. Run and run as fast as I can and the animalman is ahead so fast this powerman.

Run!

Mannis power my legs. Me with the man who has everything.

A farm with homemade wine to dine

Run!

plants that you can smoke.

Run!

and a cold shower for when your insides grow too big. The rub my feet in the sand kick off your shoes liberation. Pump pump pump of my happyheart!

Quel Pays!

SPLASH! Crash! Merrymermaid eyes her longlost lover.

I love him. I loved him. I can feel him now. Hands of the Prince. Sand of the desert saltythighs. Free. We reach the sea me and the man who has everything. Hurl ourselves into the deepblue oceansea.

You are dolphin. You are like me. You are free.

Free like a butterfly free like a bee. These are the words of my Granddaddy.

Save yourself from the seven deadly sins! Come and see the woman unchained!

My grandmother stern handsome and proud dragged through Hyde Park in chains. And I Mannis unravel unchain myself Houdini style from the Catherine Wheel of past fortune. The Wheel. The union three and then four and then one. Houdini escape nicking licking the key from the tongue of his loved one. As they kissed.

We kiss for as long as a drive through America through Nevada

Through SA-ha-ra. See SA-ha-ra.

Be SA-ha-ra.

The Kiss

Deep as dolphins smile

Wide as love can reach

Warm as the first flame

The beginning of a fantastic voyage

Deep and wide and warm electric shockcharged through my bornagain body. Chemical chaos. The Will to make two three.

And the dolphinman. He kisses me so hard and we are AdamandEve naked and we knew. He is dangerously skyhigh alive and scubadives at night so far down until his beautiful tower hardens and strengthens and pumps the sexblood. Breathing in and out. Pumping hard as the firmfarm ground we lie down on. We make the beast with two backs as his maddog howls and chases his tail till the morning.

A CUNNING LINGUIST

Where was I? Cat got your tongue says the Berber boy.

My tongue takes me back to Paris.

Tongue: a blunt tapering muscular soft fleshy organ situated on the floor of the mouth.

A deep narrow part of the current of a river, running smoothly and rapidly between rocks.

Frenchmen are great lovers. The tongue is the key. The tastes they revere. They can go into your oystercunt and out licking the whitejuice from inside you. The purecrisp joy of whitelinen cloth to nestle on your lap while the snails and pigeons and horses slither slowly down your insides. Dressed up trussed up beauties tempting your saliva to drip drip drip in the richred I feel fine full wine poured with nectarlove saved only for angels.

Look at your eyes you are an angel.

Food for thought as Babette's feast grabs hold and enfolds me with its sheer intoxication. A trouble shooter I of charm to disarm even the most difficult character. An English lesson with the most fastidious little Belgian truffle I have ever seen. His desires to be on the silver screen tarnished by the varnish on the crème brulée to which he now competes with to become the smoothest Maître D in the whole of France.

Face to face head to head in tippity top Paris hotel with the Hercule Poirot midget wanting an expert to aid him in his culinary contest. He gets me. Expert bullshitting queen.

Silver-tongue show in the plush hotel with Monsieur Buiron. We have coffee on a silver tray and decide to work on his fluency.

Tongue tied he is not. AngloSaxon fish and chips me lost in a sea of eating etymology. My Angel delight plight. Baked beans and Batman will not impress this shortstumped mealymouthed man and with all my might I act like impressed with the bestdressed Maître D in gay Paree. He asks me if I know what a truffle is and I remember the xmas xcitement Terry's All Gold Christmas box .

Just one each!

I remember the picture of the Cherry Fancy and Oh! Cream Tangerine Montélimar but we have to have them all pulled out to do the Savoy Truffle. I got class me.

Mais bien sûr monsieur it's a chocolate?

He is supershocked beyond belief surrounded by munching-morons in his ivory kitchen tower.

Mais non! Ç'est pas ça!

The disbelief of the food chief pumped up peacock high this tiny sly guy. He jumps off his chair like a meercat only 12 inches high aware of the need to educate us port and lemon English custard curd melons. It's all rhubarb to me as he leads me to the kitchen and lines the waiters up to pass the precious jar of truffles. Handled with such care these gems of the soil passed along the line. Uranium precious. Explosive earthdust. The richest delicacy that the pigs sniff out. My inside wants to scream BUT THERE ARE PEOPLE STARVING IN AFRICA. As he lifts the silver lid off the jar and sticks the truffles under my nose. The whole stuffing staff wait with fishbaited breath.

One shaving is worth a thousand pounds.

Right oh so I guess there are two kind of truffles

Oui Mademoiselle Oui!

The Freakish frog and The Mad Cow. Only the French in the

midst of national food crisis. Vache folle. Curdling fromage. Only the French government could come up with the seven year truffle plan. Save the truffle!

I was the Pigman's truffle but he couldn't eat me whole. Just shavings. Scrapings off the skinsurface. Rarebreed truffle. He dug his knife down into the earth and the tip scratched the truth truffle but did not manage to penetrate this edible diamond. I. No they can't take that away from me.

I leave the hotel with a smile inside and out and spring hits me smack bang in the face. Crocus peep their hopeful rainbow arrows up and gay Paris dances within me. My heart is light and high as the peak when the tower is so far inside you. You are full and whole.

Mannis my petit mimi my chou my grenouille my darling my my my. Be mine. I see her in her studette. Typing. Just a glimpse of her golden hair and I care so much. She cannot see me she does not know how my blood doth flow again. I will give her all my soul she must never need for anything. This woman. I lie beside my wife and the dreams they are now in English. My black and white shell now smells of English roses and country gardens in many colours. The English rose growing red. Blooming but pricked when touched. I love her more than words can say. So this is love. If only the wicked witch was dead. But she lies snoring beside me. Roaring the life from me. My tower has lost its power. Mannis Poor. She stirs the foundations of my limp flaccid world. I am not so old but no longer of the sexual world. Impotent wanderer.

SLEEP

1a The naturally recurring (esp. nightly) condition of repose and inactivity assumed by people and most higher animals in which conscious response to external stimuli and voluntary muscular action are largely suspended.

2d a complete absence of noise bustle; silence

Three to four in the numbcold morning. Sleep is brokenawoken at this time when human us are most likely to die as our body slows down and rests in a near anaesthetic darkness. The not-so-old man awakes with appalling regularity at this doomsday hour when the brainblood trickles to a very near halt. EinSteintime. The faster things go the smaller they are and at this slow doe hour I Mannis Poor appear larger than life.

I see her light on. She arrived tonight with a man in a long red coat whirling through the courtyard spinning around on a mysterious black chair. Like Boudicca on her chariot. I can hear the music she is playing escaping through her ceiling and he must be touching her creamy oyster soft thighs and his human huge hands rubbing her inside and out. Wet whiteness filling her deserted insides.

And I lay legs apart for all to see. Pushing them so far that I can feel you inside. Just in and your tongue licks and tickles. The shaved Frenchhead with the tattooed bulldogskin lies between my legs. The spring heralding the arrival of the Africansummer. In my small hands I have the whole world. Looks like a baby down there. Moustached muncher skilled in touching and taunting the glorywave. Sending me victorious. Happy and glorious bolted and throbbing againandagain. Thankyou. Thankyou. Perverse violence to reach this high and I am going too far. I went too far.

She always goes too far.

And the Berber Prince lays me down in warm African blankets in the farstarry night and takes me further to a place I still could not face and love is made. The young lean body follows biology deep and plasticprotection of the Western clinicalcynical safesexual bedsit world feels like oil in a tajine. He spins me solar wise to the dunemoon and back to a land of blankbliss. A kiss in the nick of time saving me from the not-so-old man who stole something that summer. The summer that is coming after the crocus spring and the bloody butcher. And the dolphins.

The black chair is still there but I have gone. Could not stay in the notsogay petite studette in Avenue Dosh. Money Money Money must be funny in a rich man's will. Could not stay after the summer. The not-so-old man listens to her breathing in and out. Money tap tap on the creamyflap.

Qu'est ce que ç'est la chaise noire?

Black chair hair of the dog and the neighbours muse over La anglaise who came crashing in at neardawn. Viking Queen on her newly found black leather chariot.

DREAMHOLE

Dream-hole: definition (now rare) as referring to holes by which the sound of bells escaped. An opening in an outside wall of a church tower, barn etc

Where was the not-so-old man to find his dreamhole where his music could escape. To find a crack in my outside wall. A small opening that once entered could be made larger. One touch of my foot. Human hand left there a second too long. The villa in the south. Suntanned skin glowing gold angel sent from paradise. I love the sun and little darling here it comes. Hard. Beating on my sinfulskin. I am good in my skin. Je suis bien dans ma peau but his skin is too big for him hanging off his boneframe and so to the summer where the not-so-old man sheds his skin. Thou shalt not kill hearteater.

Parisien. My prison and rich little poor Mannis seduced into kindness. The studio seacabin where each night I climb to the bed of double loneliness screaming for some justice and the whitenight fear of nothing and money makes the world go round. Selling my time to others so why not sell my time to the not-so-old man. Masturbation fantasy where I am spanked like Colette by Willy from a Paris of old and the not-so-old man ratatat taps on my heavy door. Time for a lesson. He enters proper and right. The not-so-old gentleman. Teacherrole control but like I said before. There's no room for bores or cheats and to teach it means to listen.

Listen. Listen. Easy to say. Hard to do and the not-so-old man cannot manage it anymore. Suffered so many fools notsowell and with age the body cage drops and the tongue is released full force coarse and I know best. I am the captain right or wrong and so you are. So you are. He talks and drills me with sounds of anal frustration to my rude AngloSaxon tongue. So inside this French

J'ai vu.Non. Vu.Non. Vu. Vu...ooouuouuuo..

Talk until I'm blue into space in the face. I become deaf and dumb. You fall into my eyes that I can't hide. Enjoying your power and watching my lips redripe as so fine wine and...

Just once more Mannis take the sound in then out in and out.

So proper yet later in my nightporn vision. Masturbation release. I need to sleep so trapped am I by desire. I want to feel hands slip up my little skirt that I wear in my fantasy eyes and touch my inside lips so wet. Just touch and make me plead for a fullflesh fuck inside me. I cry and beg. Turn me around and take me from behind. Hold my hips like a dog and pierce me with love.

I am a protestant says the not-so-old man and I think of those damn missionaries spoiling all the fun insisting on everyone lying flatback and thinking of England. Missing it missionary position. Get up on all fours take it from behind but the old man is teaching me French from the front. Fourchet no the r it comes right from the back of your deepthroat.

r r ar arrr AHHH fourrrchet. Je suis fourchet. I'm broke.

I'm sure you are. I want to help.

He offers to pay the rent that is then sent in the same cleanwhite envelope up to the third floor landlady who is his femme. Deception on a grand scale and I see her in the morning. Walking the Japanese bundle of powdered violence. Oh spoilt dog and she bids me a Bonjour. Tiredlooking. A woman of money and material who gave her spirit to gold and old relics of past jewelled-glory and now losing the one man she can hold.

Losing him as he slips into the spinning reel of Mannis Poor.
Obsession is my speciality.

THE SOMMELIER

The not-so-old man's wife is becoming increasingly suspicious and I decide 'tis time to move. An apartment in Montmartre with the help of the not-so-old man's big fat deposit. A perfect Last tango in Paris apartment complete with a spying avuncular concierge. The local bar on my street looks like it's from the set of Amélie. The reds and oak woods light up the night. Beatrice Dale and Sting live on my street. Not too shabby here. Betty Blue returned from her desert fire. I walk in and the first person I see is the bar man. Tallblond and handsome with a Gaulish manner reminiscent of a French film star.

Mademoiselle

He offers me white wine to taste and I am delighted to discover this barman at my new local. He is friendly gregarious miles away from the dour faced Parisiennes in other bars oozing charm like garlic dripping from the bread he is making. Christophe has very little English and communicates with offerings of more wine and flicking peanuts in my direction as his eyes twinkle. Clowning around like this his friends say he has a heart of gold but no woman has yet won it.

The day I decide to wear a skirt to teach English to the heads of Chanel, Lindt andGivenchy, he notices. He asks me to come out with him for oysters the next Sunday. His only day off. I accept. Sunday comes but it is raining. The Sommelier insists he will not take me on his bike in the rain. He thinks I may fall or the bike may skid.

C'est dangereux

Each Sunday comes and goes and each Sunday it rains. Now

I am full of curiosity about this charming man and pray for April sunshine. Finally three Sundays down the line the sun rises up over the Sacré Coeur. He rings on my doorbell helmet in one hand and flowers in the other. He helps me onto the bike. Gleaming and majestic machine full of roar and promise. He is dressed in black and I sit behind him holding on for dear life. The engine starts up and we race through the streets. The bike slips roars and slides through Paris. Marianne Faithful would be proud as I ride through Paris with the warm wind in my hair better than a sports car any day. We reach the Baron Rouge. A biker's bar unlike I have ever seen and feast on oysters and crisp white wine off his bike saddle. No Hells Angels in sight. A group of his friends join us and Christophe holds me close to him. His smell is pungent and releases pure nectar in me, it smells like teen spirit and teenage kicks. I can't stop staring at him, it feels like we are one. He is a true Frenchman. Peasant garlic soaked hands and wine-rich fleshy lips. Romance and scent. His voice is deep strong and true and when he speaks my skin tingles and I shudder a little. The oysters slide down with the taste of the sea and the body born. His eyes are Newman- blue like mine. But they hold much more depth than Newman's piercing cool gaze. These eyes are warmer full of love for the world's sensuality.

He prepares the oysters with shrewd attention to detail. His Swiss Army knife lives in his back pocket with his Marlboro reds. His big hands open the white wine and he pours me a glass. The texture is smooth.

Comme ta peau

Your skin is so soft. He says as he smells the wine. His nose is sensitive as a raw wound. He is kind and at first I am unsure but he kisses me so tenderly and caresses me so I feel like spun gold.

He feeds me the oysters and the afternoon's pleasure intensifies. I feel like I have stepped into a Parisian painting, warmth, wine and ripe women. We spend the afternoon locked in this suspended time and as the sky begins to fall on our heads we speed back through Paris down the necks of Hausmann's starry city, holding him as tight as I can with my hands gripping his hard metal belt.

Back at the flat in the hallway he kisses me hard. He lifts my skirt and slowly feels me deep inside. I am bleeding but it does not faze him. I know this will be good. I can sense his absolute exactness with food and wine will be executed on me. My legs are weak beneath me as we head for the bedroom. He lies me on the bed and takes off my shirt then bra. I am shaking all over and the room is cold. I feel his cock up against my stomach it is long and full of untold promise. I smile at him as he rubs himself up and down me. I am wet as the oyster cunts I just ate and fit to crying. Now he enters me hard and fast then slowly and tenderly. The Viking blood is flowing out of me as I come wave after wave of intense pleasure. The mixing of blood and sperm and his jewel blue eyes which are so open and raw and this is true love we are making with our sex.

He moves down my body licking the flesh. A sensualist-taster. He is drawn to my body intoxicated by the deep lilac wine. His hands used to chopping and serving now prepare me impeccably through every fingertip. I feel so close to love. We light up like seahorses as he pours wine into my mouth.

We kiss. French kisses exchanging the smooth mead between us licking mouths tongues and faces. There is blood everywhere and he goes down and starts to taste my deep red wine. I see his mouth blood red like his lips and the savage in him springs to life. He is earthy and real. A peasant brought up on a farm watching the animals mate and give birth with the blood and the sweat and the pain. He moves up towards my mouth and enters me full force hard as a bull and kisses me. Crosses my lips with blood as he presses deep inside me. I come again and again without moving. I cling to him this man. For that is what he is.

A man.

Remember. Frenchmen are great lovers. The tongue is the key. The tastes they revere. They can go into your oystercunt and out licking the whitejuice from inside you. The purecrisp joy of whitelinen cloth to nestle on your lap while the snails and pigeons and horses slither slowly down your insides. Dressed up trussed up beauties tempting your saliva to drip drip drip in the richred I feel fine full wine poured with nectarlove saved only for angels.

The doorbell rings and I remember I have a date with my benefactor richy rich sugar Daddy who wants to wine and dine me. Christophe is asleep so I let Daddy in. He has roses in one hand and fresh oysters in the other. I try to hide the helmet as he confronts me in the tiny kitchen. His eyes are huge with excitement and he presses against me. He leans forward to kiss me and as I duck out the way the helmet is revealed.

Whose is this?

Oh it's just the barman's.

He looks displeased at the sight of the helmet. He has told me before of his fear of motorbikes roaring up behind him in the South of France. The black helmet of virility hunting him down. I know you have your needs he says to me. I don't want to let him down he has been so good to me so I leave Christophe sleeping and head out with Daddy for some more oysters.

In his car he rests his hand on my knee and lets it drift a little too far up my skirt.

I am so happy to see you Mimi.

He is nearly 70 years old and gets such a thrill from the smallest titillation so I allow him to flirt a little. In the restaurant he feeds me oysters. I am pretty drunk by now so high on the day and eager to return to Christophe praying he is still sleeping. As we drive back I am as high as a ten tequila night in anticipation of the pleasure to come. I kiss Daddy goodbye as he holds me against him a little too long.

C'est les petits bonheur qui fait les grands bonheur

It's true and today is full of little pleasures and what the French call little deaths. I return and undress sliding back beside Christophe ready for another death. He is hard and just about to wake, he kisses me and penetrates me from behind.

Faire l'amour faire l'amour

I am ecstatic driven wild by my own need. At first it hurts and I can't understand how anyone can manage this pain but he slides back and forth making it wetter with the oyster he has hooked on his finger, which he gradually inches inside my behind. I am shaking badly. This feeling is the most I have ever known, overwhelming in its intensity. He is some way in and he puts the sheet between my teeth as if to silence my whelping.

Strange animal noises escape my lips as he pushes deeper and deeper in. Tears now as he lifts my body upwards like a cobra rising up and very gently strokes my skin. The pain and the lightness of touch the ripping and the care makes me shudder and cry out as he then begins to thrust back and forth harder and harder until I think I may die from this feeling of ultimate union. He comes inside my arse and like a spent lioness I am tossed to the side curling up feeling more alive than I have in years. Lying looking out at the Parisian night.

I feel the warm burn turn cold under the watchful gaze of the Sacred Heart. I am glad I was born a lover.

L'ILE DESERT

As the spring passes its bursting baton to summer I hope summer catches it. It does. I walk in desertdreams. So soon I can traveltime. But here and now in France. I am locked away in weekend workshops looking for l'île déserte with the International troupe de théâtre. We act a play. A group of office workers trapped in the basement for years. Performing seals. Silently yelping repetitive tasks. Built to last our lifesentence time. Us. Vibrant players barked at by the Chef and the mad Coca-cola swigging chain-smoking God bless America for these sugar candy goodies Frenchfrank director. He bespectacled intellectual tyrant. Puts us through our paces. We work in a room with no windows. The method can drive you right out of yourself. The playworkers. They moved office seven years ago from the basement to the seventh floor where they can see the Navire the maudit navire qui va et vient. The ships that come and go. They can see the world outside and have never taken the boat that wails and hails its departure all day as they stay inside themselves. Locked under neon light. Twisted distorted selves craving to be Tout Nu. Nu. Nude.

Naked. definition 1 Of the body or part: unclothed. stripped to the skin. not covered or protected by clothing.

Nude. bare. stripped. exposed. unclothed. au naturel. without a stitch on. in ones birthday suit. in the raw. in the altogether. in the buff. naked as the day one was born. mother naked. buck naked.

Quel pays! Nous allons trouver l'île déserte!

Honey sweet take me to paradise. We search for the paradise island every weekend locked inside the smells and funny other faces and together we share the aim to liberate and create a dance where all can join. Young. Old. Fat. Thin. Uglybeauty. Feeling this pulse. Blood-running sex. All unite in bringing our insides out. Spill our guts and lusty love for all. Chestbeating rhythm. We make a boat from a table and magic carpets win Swallows and Amazon style. We dance hard but we cannot release our crushed Western insides. We cannot flower.

Act we try. Imagine we lie. Naked Liars. Sucking coconuts and making love in the seasands. Hands all hands. Workers I see you as you read. Maybe you're inside a train and looking out and hating the sheep following herd but the pain of walking the other away against the tide of Eliot-described zombie workers deprived of light driven underground travel. You screw your braininsane so downthedrain its large great rainbow-matter that they tell you is grey. Cannot question the purpose of the facts and figures they manoeuvre each day come what may and so they introduce duvet day. A world where the only escape is under the covers inside your warm-torn self but don't stay too long or you'll be on the dole. Rocknroll.

The brain: the organ as the seat of sensation. motion or human speech. the organ of thought. memory or imagination; in pl. intellectual power. intellect. thought. sense. imagination.

Informal. highbrow. egghead. Einstein.

Time.

THE HOSPITAL

The hospital tucked away in bourgeoise decay and come what may the not-so-old man is becoming hip again. A brand new hip hip hooray operation so he can movesmooth again.

Hanch hip in French

Colloquial: *déhanchement* French for sexgrind.

With my new hip and patched-up heart I am captain right or wrong.

The anaesthetic puts him under into a world of dreams. He dreams of Mannis. Me. Mannis Poor.

Anaesthesia: absence of sensation; esp. artificially induced inability to feel pain.

The not-so-old man's dream.

I dreamed that the world was a very large garden
But the wind awoke me
Bringing red petals flying in the night
Their perfume was sweet and subtle
The silk of their skin like satin
Slowly a face showed among them
Little by little a young woman appeared
I looked at the sky and saw one of the stars
Coming to me. She was bright and delicately
Spread her light and heat over the young lady
I, then, knew who they were and why
My hottest love was devoted to them.
I said "stay with me, you are my life".
I long for the Garden and the Sky.

I promised to visit the moneyman and where are the four loving children? Too busy with their new families composing the tune to their third mobile phone wrapped up in their spool-spoiled selves and do not want to delve into whiteglove tearfear of Daddy's doom. Besides he was never there when I I I needed him so he can go to hell but smell the money. It is in no jeopardy.

I think of my Dad and he is simply the best so I must go visit the failed Father. The late lover. So on a sunshot soon to be thirty day. I take a bus to leafy green so quiet surburban stillness stillborn day. Hospitals all white light and life-death dedication to beat beat beat the decay and the beat beat beat of the not-so-old man's heart and rage rage rage against the dying of the light.

I climb stair after stair head throbbing and certain someone will grab me X-ray me tell me I have everything Ebola, vache folle, hepatitis a b c d eeeasy does it Mannis and maybe they will keep me inside this white life-death cloud and never let me out where the sun slashes the trees and beauty brings you to your knees.

Breathe. Mannis. Breathe... keep breathing and at the top I see a corridor of whitelight and a gagglegash of giggling nurses.

Qu'est-ce que vous voulez?

I want to see the not-so-old man but they don't understand and are laughing so hard at me. My flushing face outside burns inside and I stumble over French names and want to run run away. Far far away. Into the desert.

The nonsolid man hop skips and jumps to my rescue graspsgasps for his ironstick crutches as I Mannis Poor appear bright flesh and blood crutch. Love. So chirpy chipper this Anglophile mischievously imp-faced Santa Clause. Pale as a poleaxed polar bear left on crushed ice and

Oh! Mannis you're so nice to have come.

Tears well up in the not-so-old man's eyes of hope and visions of his Southern Serenity Paradise where he can find his sealegs again and find the dolphin in me that could eventually drown him.

I stay less than long and race down the stairs to the bus that takes me to the building where I can swim. I pass the femme of the not-so-old man on the steps of the white careshare hospital. She smiles fit to crack her made-up face and who made it up and why am I there before the conjugal role-regal one. She thinks I'm the mistress and what games people play to make it through the day and Who is afraid of …?

Swim. Mannis. Swim away the disease. The death breath. You are dolphin.

You are free.

Water spares me of all worry. I swim. The light and dark make sense and my head in and out of the water escapes the heavyhospital. Flipping fickle fish fintailing my mood into lightmight. Come what May. I'm the captain right or wrong.

Lead us not into temptation and deliver us from evil. Blood pumping in my ears through my body.

PUMP! PUMP! PUMP !

Bodyblood. Through the body. Drive. Force. Push. Send.

The not-so-old man spent his glorydays pumping oil from the dryrich desert. Sucking wealth from the African world pumping the global petroleum fatcats with francs. He and Charles de Galle caught in a snap sniffing the rich addictive oilsyrup in the slippery Colonial past. Charlie gave a faint smile away from his elephant face and with a wry raised Gaullish brow declares:

C'est le vin du pays!

The photo black and white captures the not-so-old man laughing so hard Oh LA! LA! LA! LA! LA! LAAA!

AHHHHHH!

Here before now. I need to tell you. In my Gertrude Stein Eisenstein time. The summer before this desert. The one I wanted to tell you that firstburst through this blankscape desertwhite pagetime..

Tis Time.

BULLETLINES

Here in the desert I travel on the Desert Prince's camel. He protects me from the scorpions. I love these dunemoons sinking soft in the sand. Moulding time in curves.

Horizon gazing at empty hours.

The heatdry vision screams inside my head and shoots me back to linear time. Greenwich Meantime. Mean time. Mean.

TGV bulletlines from Paris to Toulon. Straight rock hard metallic force shunting me forwards dressed to kill.

The bending rising and falling of sandtime.

So now the summer is coming. In sickness and in health. For better for worse. Till death us do part.

An invitation to Serenity villa the sumptuous lure of a taste of the good life. In your dreams you've been here. Swimming to the bar. A star in search of a cocktail umbrella to suck suck this lucky life.

As the train rushes forward I start to dream.

Train-rocked and sun-warmed searching searching for black bras and each time I find one it becomes a blackcat attacking strangling me gripping and clawing at my neck until I awake screaming. I strangled by my sexual potency or an Irish memoir. Nina Simone who lives down in the South keeps a gun to shoot at anyone disturbing her peace.

Black cat cross my path. I think everyday is gonna be my last.

Here before now. I need to tell you. In my Gertrude Stein Eisenstein time. The summer before this desert.

The one I wanted to tell you that firstburst this blankscape desertwhite pagetime.

Tis time.

THE SUMMER

Purples and pinks and shades and cocktail umbrella drinks and Chanel stinking rich St Tropeztray of pastis drunk on the terrace where the summer begins. Texaschain friends. Morallysawed redmassacre turned to blackblood mascara dripping down the cheeks of the facelifted oilbaroness whose sheephusband sleeps as she turns the other cheek in her chainmail dress and the not-so-old woman can buy buy buy her youth. Oil herself back to life tinman style. Iron out the creases so from the outside all is right while inside rustsbusts imploding in a cry. An O! A wooden O!

And me Mannis rich little poor girl. Empowered. Accept the invitation South from the not-so-old man.

Tickets sent in the post to toast me up for the eating. Fattening her up and baste her in the scorching sun. And Mummy and Daddy can come too.

Plans are made and my bullet train arrives a few lucky lucky hours before the others. Greeted me with salmon and rosé and he dressed to impressed like a millionaire yacht man. Pretty in pink. Neck as high as a giraffe ready for the extra pumping. Awaiting the arrival of Mum and Dad and my oldest childhood friend Ella. The cast assembling for the summer.

I have the feeling I am meeting my in-laws.

The not-so-old man stands in his masterbuilt villa after the summer or is it before. He is nearly 70. He is in love with me. He misses me. Mannis. A girl remember not a woman. Un garcon manqué.

A tomboy. A missing boy.

Your soft voice is missing
Your blue smile is vanishing
In the darkness of the deepsea
I try to perceive your perfume
Among the ghosts of your presence
Oh! My dearest
Where is my deepest love?
Where is my charming lady?
Where and to whom is she engaged?
What fate and doom and what for?
Which devil is taking her away?
Where is she? Why?
Oh! My Dearest
The nightlights of the bay are twinkling
Like thousands of little stars
And the sunbeams are caressing the sleeping flowers
And the silence of the night
Invades my soul and Being
But the lighthouse out in the dark sea
Sends me hope and comfort
Its lightbeams are hundreds of messages
From my dearest's soul and mind
Let all good be with you. Sleep quietly.
In spite of all demons and fears
I love you.

Eat your heart out cynical youth. Byronic age reigns here. Let it come down.

Waiting on the platform. My parents appear excited and confused but soon wooed by the charm. There's no harm in taking from the rich if you're Robin Hood poor. Stuck in front of the smelly telly asking ten times a day. Who wants to be a millionaire? Seduced by thousands of images to make life seem elsewhere. The advertising crushes and grinds our here and now. Retarded retailers reduced to a quintessence of dust.

After Three is Four. A quintessence of dust.

We must have goods goods goods to feel happy. Life reduced to a prize winning view holiday for two here to Kathmandu. We know you want. The pool. The sun. The car. The house. The DVD. For better or worse. Better better quality. A digital photobooth multiple choice selection to improve yourself to perfection. Boxed affection to encourage the erection. Heart-sectioned. To have is to hold. I want. I want. I want. And here a dream come true. A holiday for two in the South of frisky France. All expenses paid. Shelling out the money like he was about to die. And you can really sell your soul. Ain't that funny!

Waiting at the station for those who borewhore me and I love them. Take a breath for England Mannis you can do it. Here they come greeted by the pink shirted honey man who can treat them to all the ice-creams in the van.

I hired a car. Only the best.

Opentop success. Wind in our hair blowing away the cares of who will pay pay pay. A dream holiday come true. Especially for you two who created my angel. My Mannis. All he wants to do is thank them for putting me on this earth. For letting him feelreel slippery as an eel again. Reeling us in.

We drive through the cricketrickit night. As warm as lovejuice when it first explodes. As right as that night when you loved so nearclear. The warmwind in all our hair and thank the world for the summer. Where would we be without it? Suicidal. Vodkasoaked Nordic on the clink brink or blackened oppressed treacle tarts. Like pain. You forget the sun when it's not there. I mean you want it. Craverave it but never really recall it. Feeling so small in your cold bones. Oh when stone heartwinter passes and summer wind washes you throughout in the opentop openshop haylight. Strawbeams into our skin and wins the night from us. And Dad so pleased to be back at ease in the bosom of wealth. Stolen from him by the stealthy dodgy business partner who flew flew flew the cuckoo's nest and left Dad abreast of things to cry weep wail on Mama's breast to test the strongest bond of marriage carriage clockstop. And here and now we all drive into the paradise world. A world where no matter what happens you never have to pay. Mannis in wonderland. Grand and nothing to pay.

What mad Nijinsky wrote
about Diaghilev
Is true of the normal heart
For the error bred in the bone
Of each woman and each man
Craves what it cannot have.
Not universal love
But to be loved alone

We must love one another or die yet old Auden changed this to *and* die as he grew cold not so bold older.

And the not-so-old man feeling not so cold now must love me or die. All the fine feasting leads to an omen. A sighting of a dolphin out on the yacht as I the captain right or wrong steer us into the oceanblue. A drop of gold in his eye. Slowly sipping the vin du pays. Merry and gay. We lounge on the yacht trotting along to the sillysound. Jingle jangle of gold coins dropping like pebbles in the sea. The old triangle. 3. You are dolphin. You are like me.

Where do you think you are your father's yacht?

I gaze at the sea where the old sailor will soon lie and I know I must return to The Pigman. The dolphin rises high splashing joy across the sky. Majestic. Beautiful. Flashing smile. A mile of happiness in one face. I see it was me. Long long ago. Miles and miles and smiles away. My soul as old as centuries. Before the parasites came to feed on my fertile flesh. Ransacking my lighthouse. Kidnapping my golden years.

Building us up to fever pitch. Me myself and I. My so precious special Ma and Pa and childhood friend drinking champagne on the terrace of the villa. The killerthriller villa where all day the not-so-old man has devoted his being to marinating us into the best lamb curry we have ever had. The food seduces all our souls as the mistral crawls inside us. The gullible gulls.

GULLIBLE: credulous, trustful, over-trustful, easily deceived, easily taken in, unsuspecting, unsuspicious, ingenuous, naive, innocent, simple, inexperienced, green, foolish, silly, wet behind the ears. Antonyms: cynical, suspicious.

The seagulls glide and soar rinsing the hotsun from their uneasy featherwings maddened by the Mistral. Present and hovering for days. Waiting for the right time to winsin under our skin and the music plays on.

I got you deep in the heart of me.

The Mistral begins to blow fullforce. To blow all the cobwebs and days of pain from the old man who is feeling so light and young again as he entertains what he maintains to be his in-laws. The mistral. The mistress of winds that led Van the painter man to slice off his very own ear. They say le mistral comes in threes. If it blows the fourth day then it could last six. I start feeling queer. If it persists till the seventh it will last for nine. Swinging on the summerswing with my bare feet on the seat next to him as we laugh and giggle. My Dad says that winds disturb men's minds. Their very own menstrualmistral tension and he withdraws to his room. Wise in his own spirit and definitely bien dans sa peau. Ella has a smoke and retires tired from the wind and the old man's war stories repeated in cycles. Cyclones of anticlockwise memory back and forth till you're inside out with listening. Verbal torture people subject you to. To bed. To bed and who would have thought the old man to have so much blood in him.

On the terrace we sat. The woman who brought me up and the not-so-old man who brought me down to his meddle level. A guardian angel and a devil in disguise. Brandy handed out by the randy scout. My Ma and me find the wind exciting. Lightening our hearts. Tripping though life. Joyous with the deadlydigestive going down nicely. The last sip before I truly become a maneater. Chewing them up.

The wind is howling now. Now. The summer. The one I wanted to tell you about on this white escape page. The trees bending and it feels like an ending and beginning and the not-so-old man's head starts spinning towards Shelley quoting quoting.... *No sister flower would be forgiven*...as he looks at his Captain Bird's Eye view.

If it disdained its brother
The beauty of the World hurts
And the sunlight clasps the earth;
and then suddenly
And the moonbeams kiss the sea
so suddenly
What is all this sweet work worth
His hand touches
If thou kiss not me?
my foot.

I let it rest for just a few seconds too long. Just long enough to feel the man within returning. All it takes is a few seconds to send laser beams to the pumping penis heart and he is born again. I turn. I yearn for some sexual love. Some belonging not felt for so many moons. The Man who had everything. The lover's piano hands. I forget myself and then I remember. I say goodnight and he follows hoping for a nightcap in our masterbedroom like the night before. Pushing himself through the door into possible girlsworlds where the legs glisten and the honeysmile door opens.

Can I come to your room?

No

No is good, 'no' is the right answer for me. Not for him. I see his face in the mistralmoonlit night and all is not right. The madness in his eyes is clear as deaddeer blood and Oh Mannis what inferno have you released. I run down the steps and lock the door behind me. I telephone a friend who wants to be a millionaire style. Then out of the mistralwhistling air my best friend releases a horrorscream. Screaming to heaven her delicate lungs.

What?!

We stop and listen. He wails King Lear prose into the night.

Blow winds blow and crack thy cheeks…

He is wheezing...moaning and groaning.

WHY! WHY! WHY!

Out we rush and I believe he is dying from a heart rack a tack tack attack. He speaks wild whirling words something is rotten in his ghostly core.

I always get what I wanted. I'm the captain right or wrong.

We. Terrified eyed go to him. I hang back knowing I to be the cause of his soulpain. Me. Mannis The King's jester. Smiler. Telling touching truths. The comic conman. The friendly fool. Ella tries to calm him down.

She would be with me if it wasn't for Ann-Marie she would be with me I know I know...

No she wouldn't. She is young. You're too old for her. She has her whole life ahead of her.

I slink inside ashamed of the games we play. Visions of tabloid news. Bloody headlines. 4 SLAYED IN LUXURY VILLA. I am panicking now and I phone a friend again and I hear my x x x lover's constant richrolling through the years velvetvoice. I also hear a scream. Piercing me inside out. Curdling. Rolling from Ella's lipslungs.

Oh my God! He is naked dancing naked outside the window. He he he.....

The shock of the body. Tout nu. The old body with the skin grown too big and the heart too small and what is this creation made. A design so gloriously right yet so repulsively recklessly wrong and the not-so-old man has seen his own reflection. Lines drawn that cannot be rubbed out. Erased. And in the reflection. Me. Mannis. The révélateur. The revealer. Me. The shock of the new. He rattles and rails around his masterbuilt house. Shouting.

This is my house !

For the error bred in the bone of each man and each woman craves what it cannot have.

I have fear this time. Whiteknuckle heart racing terror. I grab two iron rods placed on the desk. We cannot see well. The dark and mistralmood plain petrify our myopic minds. We have no time to place plastic disks in our shattered eyes. We rely on instinct. I tell my friend if you see him hit him. I know he has cracké. Cracked. Crossed over. This. Is. It. And that was that.

We run to Mum and Dad who are making love to the winds and as always there is beauty magic and truth. We run but he stops me from behind. Towelclad. Angry blue Van Gogh eyes. No lies. I turn. I thrash his head with my iron rod. Me. Mannis Poor. Learning from. Rising from the cinders of neanderthal man's ashes. Ruby in the dust. He hits the ground gurgling and burbling sounds. Pleading to dance with me. Swim with me.

You are my dolphin. Little dolphin. Let's go to the sea. You too are like dolphin. You are like me.

We scramble down his front garden full of exotic spikes and shade. He never takes this path anymore as his hip will not allow it. Damnable body. So miraculously Herculean. Now so tired and weak. He will not take this path again. There is blood pouring from the gash in his head. The gashcunt did it.

I follow him down the slippery slope and we reach the beach where the mountains meet the sea and all things by law divine.

Mannis in one spirit meet and mingle why not I with thine?

Oh! Mannis please touch me. Please eat me so it is not the worms that take my flesh. I want you this way.

I headclear what to do and I strip off my clothes as my breasts shine in the moonlight and I sing to this not-so-old man. I take him in my not-so-old arms and I rub myself against him. His heart pump pump pumps so fast as we advance into the warm water. I am a fantasy free dolphin. I swim underwater searching for the withered life force and begin to tickle and lick him back to life. He is breathing hard and eyes twinkling at the moon. I press myself against his oldman of the sea and I push him inside me so now there is no way out. One way ticket to heaven and what a wonderful way to die. He is rising rising splashing in the spree sea he always loved and he cannot take this much pleasure. His heart is pumped to bursting bursts inside me and now he is free. His body floats on the surface and then descends to the ocean bed. I drag him to the shore and go hunting for firewood. So hungry now. After sex. So like the black spiders who eat their sexmeat for afters.

I build a fire.

Come thick night

I hunt for a knife.

And pall thee in the dunnest smoke of hell

I begin with the fingers

That my keen knife see not the wound it makes

and then the cause of all.

Nor heaven peep through the blanket of the dark

I eat the tower of sex.

To cry hold the babyshrivelled *hold* penis pathetic sausage roll not filling enough and I gaze at the sea where the old sailor must now lie now. This ignorant present taste of porkman on my tongue and I feel now I know I must return to the pigman.

The future in the instant

But first I must finish off the legs and breast and cut out his heart because that is what I need to bury in my wilderness.

3 hearts 3 wishes 3 witches 3's a crowd

You know a good heart these days is hard to find so please be gentle with this heart of mine.

DESERT ROSE

Desert rose is the colloquial name given to rosette formations of the minerals gypsum and barite with poikilotopic sand inclusions. The 'petals' are crystals flattened on the crystallographic axis, fanning open along characteristic gypsum cleavage planes.

The rosette crystal habit tends to occur when the crystals form in arid sandy conditions, such as the evaporation of a shallow salt basin. Gypsum roses usually have better defined, sharper edges than barite roses.

The Berber woman use some medicine on me to cure me but I cannot be cured. I am like the Desert rose. Hardened in an arid sandy place for too long. Petals are crystallised and sharp now. No medicine on earth can help me now.

Like the Carrowkeel Celtic wombmound. I can build one myself to manotsokind. 3 is the magic number. 3 days the magic child will come after 3 hearts are buried. Like the Celts say.

I am Angus men call me young
I am the sunlight in the heart
Moon in the mind
I am the light at the end of every dream
I will make you immortal
For my Palace opens into the Gardens of the Sun

Dry desert days and needle pricked poked starnights to take away the sin bin. Bin so long.

Bin thinking.

I have the not so old man's hearts buried in the sand for safe keeping. Ismail has shown me a way to preserve it. Buried under my desert Rose. Still feel empty here in the desert. Feels like a quarter of my heart is missing. The empty quarter. Pigman stole it.

Stole it in that Empty bloodied Quarter.

Go back to the Pigman.

Cut out his heart.

Back to the sculptor transport his bodyparts.

Ground three hearts here in the sallowsands.

The father son and the holy ghost of man not-so-kind.

3 is the magic number.

It all comes from three.

Go back to the pigman bring back his heart.

Feed him to the pigs.

Cut out his heart in the blossom of his sin. I can see the mound in the desert. They will tell tales in the future of Mannis the Mother of Love who buried the evil hearts of men to start again. She will always be associated with pink flamingos.

Walking hand in hand with Ismail. The massive moon rolls onto my back and stars fall inside me. Sleeping with my perfect Desert Prince united in union by a ring of proud moody camels. The sex partner for the Berber starved of female flesh. Taking comfort in camels' insides until they are out of their head with desire but a blonde English girl so willing to be taken. Pressing inside me to forget my sinbin. I appear and his head is thrown.

Your eyes make my head spin. I want inside you.

No release avoidance by sucking orally that tower of strength.

That is for prostitutes I want inside you.

They want the real thing.The only raison to être is to do this in out action satisfaction and feel close to heaven on earth. That's where heaven is. On earth. Better than sex. Nothing is better nor more central inside when it is right on a Berber night. 4O days and 4O nights. I have been with the prince. I know he will help me with my heart. I draw my plan on the sand for him. I show him in pictures like my ancestors did. The back-brain instinct before the neo cortex plane came in to play and we all became so choked up on words.

I draw big hands around my neck and I mime asphyxiation. I draw a huge man and a knife with his heart out of his body. He laughs.

Then I draw a man raping me with the knife. He is ten times bigger than the girl he tries to fuck. His dick is huge and I draw a little hole which he cannot fit in. I need another way so I pick up a banana and try to push it through a small ring from the Berber woman. The pulp mashes up and drops on the sand. Finally I draw my maps to show Ismail my journey and where I want him to meet me.

Meet me in Tangiers.

I nod.

Take Care. Be Sahara. See Sahara.

It is so simple.

We kiss for as long as long can measure.

He will help me wash the stain of 2000 years of paindrain.

POISON

In the desert the Berbers show me potions mixed to heal but also to harm. I asked them you see.

What isn't known can't be stolen.

So I have learnt all about poison. I am ready now. Backwards we timespin. Desert rose rubbed out. The sins of my ancestors buried deep in the core of the earth. Sky blue new.

Memories harddrive crashing as I see burning carcasses hanging upside down. The foot and mouth crisis. Memory forcing me back to the Green Celtic land.

Playing the Queen in Hamlet.

One woe doth tread upon another's heel so fast they follow.

Do not drink Gertrude.

A cold damp house in the bogland where the wood never lights unless the Frenchman is there. He could stoke a fire from the dampest squib of a frozen night. Warming the cockles of my heart. The Big Prince not the Desert Prince. This is where we all came to play. The cast had assembled to do Hamlet and the locals became suspicious of the actors up at the White House. It is in this cold damp Withnail and I house that I meet Ophelia. Her voice warmed my Irish heart and she was young and a long way from home. Tipperary. Black rimmed glasses hiding her sea green Irish eyes ready for Ophelia's watery grave, willing to risk it all in the name of Hamlet. That deadly cold Irish winter. With extravagant costumes designed by the passionate Argentinean designer who attempted to teach us all tango for the fight scene. We played football in the evenings after rehearsals and we discovered an old candle effigy of the Virgin Mary lit in the hollow window of the back barn. We aimed to knock her off the wall by kicking the ball through the small window. One night the King was right on target and Mary was knocked off her pedestal. We laughed uncontrollably and forgot about the candle knocked into the barn full of straw. But later that evening cleaning my teeth in the freezing dank house I saw smoke pouring from the hut.

The Virgin Mary is on fire!

Me Mannis screaming my lungs out and we all take blankets to put it out and watch the smoke drift up into the cold black scarred sky punctuated with stars. Crowded starry night jostling for their space to shine. The West of Ireland. Starry skied fairy land.

I will be King and you will be Queen.

I am the Queen. I am the Queen of Denmark.

We are invited to tell our tale in the North.

As we carry disinfectant in the boot of my black car we cross to the North of Ireland. Ugly gash in the sacred land that the English planted. As we step out at the border the night guards put us through our paces. We step in the disinfectant to make sure we do not spread the cursed disease but it is not strong enough to wipe out the sins of my ancestors. I see the pillar box red colour everywhere bleeding onto their green land. How much more shame can I take. The bending winding snake roads I am used to have been straightened up by the English invaders. Stiff back. Stiff upper lip and the money machine spews out notes with the Queen on them. She looks like me. My head hurts and I feel ugly here. Strangled again. We finish the show and recover from another mass murder in the House of Denmark. Dying is an art like everything else I do it exceptional well. I do it so it feels like hell. Finally Horatio says good night to the Sweet Prince and we can all leave this stained Northern scarland. The King and Queen drive in convoy heading back to Ireland proper. The King is roaring and chasing cars up ahead strong masculine racer boy with Ophelia at his side and as I squint at the disappearing wet roads there are flashing lights up ahead. I see the police then an ambulance. More flashes. We get out of the car and see the King and Ophelia hanging upside down, bloodied bats in the racer car. Dead in a ditch. The horror.

When sorrows come they come not in single spies but in battalions.

But they were cut out and freed time turning backwards Superman style. Weren't they?

Yes. I can't remember well but please Dagda God let Ophelia be fine with children and hot cabbage and love. She really deserves it. Kind soul.

Back at the Withnail and I house we drink to kill the shockpain and at the deadzone hour of four I awake drythirst burning my insides out. I call to Hamlet for the car keys and he throws them from the top window. I scrabble around for the big tankard of water and get the rim to my mouth.

Do not drink Mannis

And just in time I realize it is the poisoned disinfectant to ward off the disease. So the Queen for now is saved but for how long.

And here in the desertsands the Berbers are teaching me all about poison. This is how I prepare for my special performance on Inish Oirr. An Island off Ireland. A perfect place to reap revenge on The Stranglar. I will be there on the night come rain or shine. Come car crashes. Poisoning. Come hell or high water. The infamous Irish swell rages over us and Hamlet turns as green as the Emerald Isle we left behind.

The water is suffocating me. Like a diver searching for lost treasure in the filthy murky sea.

Memory crashing.

Hands hurt.

Must burn this.

It does not make sense.

But the Berber women have finished their concoction.

The poison is ready now.

The next on my list is the Pigman.

He must be visited upon and then the giant Irish bear.

And no more pain for the Queen.

SEARCHING FOR THE PIGMAN

The palaces to which the Sidhe went to after fighting with the race of Mil were hidden in the depths of the Earth. The Dagda controlled the distributions of these palaces and domains. He then gave one to Lugh and retained two for himself, one of which was called Síd or Brug Maic ind Oc, which means Enchanted Palace or Castle of the Son of the Young. Mac ind Oc was a most enchanted castle that contained three trees which always bore fruit, a vessel full of excellent drink, and two pigs, one alive and the other nicely cooked ready to eat at any time; and in this palace no one ever died.

Come on down Pigman.

Driving through the Empty Quarter times spun and dug a moon around the world and back superman style. I told you the faster you go the smaller things look and here I see the shimmering whites in the eyes of the Omani Berbers that lead me like a Bethlehem star to my Inn where there was plenty of room one or a thousand summers ago. I drive back through time reaching backwards and speeding ahead. The cactus spikes are easing from my insides as I reach out my hand into the desert heatday and how I love this spacewipe time. My music tells me.

They stab it with their steely knife but they just can't kill the beast.

That won't be a problem as I walk. Alone. This time. Into the foyer of the hotel. Slabmarble whiteness brightly reflecting my sunkissed blistered beauty and the Pigman is there shooting the breeze if there was one in the staledry air. Difficult to breathe now. I check into Room 19. The same room as some summers ago. Everything is different and the same. I the flesh eater have come to take back my heart. I dress for dinner wearing white now to black out the bad. I head for the dining room for drinks with the Pigman but this time I am ready. This time I will devour him. He lumbers into the room. Same old patter. Vodkaice and a slice of your breast. He cannot recognize me now. Like a star in the galaxy much the same as another but some stand alone and here I come to reap redrevenge on you. We talk politesse and he offers to take me to see the inner desert oasis the next day. Perfectly posed in front of my victim. Not I. I will not be raped.

I sleep and dream of a garden with an old man digging but he cannot bury the two gargantuan birds who insist on resurrecting their ugly heads. One a giant black monster the other a large green grasshopper. They chase me inside my childhood home and I cannot keep them out. They sicken and disgust me and I so want to bury these eternal chasing birds.

The morning light says halo around my newmorning head and I am ready to roll the meat out into the sand. We meet, Pigman and I.

I'll bring the packed lunch.

I find some halal meat in remembrance of the pizza made tokillher. I know not to offend them. Their respect for us is so high. Pedestal pawed women in this 21st century foxy lady stoned for wearing make-up and not covering her hair. Oh not everywhere. It's just a misreading misunderstanding. But it stoned me to my soul. Stoned me just like jelly rolls. I prepare the halal meat for my man nicely seasoned. A man for all seasons is what I want. Thyme and basil and a touch of poison for the hungry Pig all stabbed on a kebab skewer. Washed down with vodka. A picnic dreams are made of.

The Pigman flirts and fawns over me. I remember the mirror of my eyes flicked down. Forced to look into my soulhole insisting I am an angel. Well here we go. Your angel is descending and ascending offering meat which he eats without question sure of a kingdom to come in his bursting brown pants. He eats and I see the roasted feast to come. I haven't eaten for days to prepare for this feast of freedom. And I take out a mirror and make him watch himself choking.

Remember me? Your angel? The one you raped? Over and over?

He shivers splutters and quakes. Heart breaking Pigman. Vigilante me. For all the courts of Arabia could not sweeten my honeysmile since this man stole my golden years. Yes I think he deserves to die.

THE FEAST

Feast. Banquet. Celebration meal. Lavish dinner. Repast. Treat. Orgy. Revels. Festivities.

I make my fire funeral pyre higher and higher and I start with his prick. Lick Lick and taste sausage and gristle. As the meat reaches inside. I feel my outside sinskin cleanse and tremble. Devour the fear in flesh. I strengthen like a Pagan Queen at her table. Tis feast time. I eat the King to snatch power from his tower and hang the leftlimbs in the Christmas tree. Daddies on the Christmas tree. But no Christmas here. So here I split the joint and hang his flesh in the datepalm trees as I enjoy piece by piece of this creature. Survival of the shittest. Not now. The tide is turning. Mannis survive I. The wittiest prettiest butterfly heart. I want my heart back as I chop away in his chest to take out his. To take back to my African desert where it all did or didn't begin. I have two hearts now and for my addictive alchemy I need the third.

3 hearts 3 wishes 3 witches 3's a crowd

3 is the magic number. 3 is better than two.

Symmetry is dangerous

3 choices

always better than two.

As I tear his thigh with my cutsharp teeth I cast my mind forwardback to the Strangular. Now he shall be visited upon and no longer shall the sins of my ancestors be visiting me.

SCULPT THE SCULPTOR

The smell of the barbequed flesh and sand in my hair I imagine sausage fingers slipping down inside me as I jetset magpie searching style back to the Emerald Isle. I drive through fields of wet damp green and feel an Emerald green sickness rising inside me as I imagine the giant Celt fall colossus-like over the cliff. I will find him in his hot tub and spike his champagne Charliesmile off his face. I use alchemy against such tritemight. Spare rib tickling me. I will take your body apart and sculpt you into pieces. Dissect. Cut up and reject. Spit out what I do not like. I and nothing. I and land and back in the desert. Old and wise. I can bury my hearts. Deep.

I will take back my fastforward life. My bloodlust pumping through my veins and here I see 2 magpies for joy on this ride of freedom. I will find the sculptor who so lickliked my neck. I will find him whole and take him home to feast with my wedding Prince. Driving through the Burren layers of ancientclockrock. Beauty grown from chalk out of this barrenland. Flowers grow. Wild fresh life. 333 . I twist and turn past the three giant tortoises. Gleaming. Greenhumped back beauty. Hunchbacklands that appear in the sea beside me and up ahead rises the sheer stoneflat beauty of Inis Oirr. That's where the sculptor resides.

Those arrogant Angles say Inisheer. Sheep sheer labyrinthine labour of hazardous stone love. Piled high wall upon wall of a mazing grace to forgive the sculptors stone hearted hands. An island no man is and as I climb the boat in Doolin Bay to find my man. I smell the water dividing me and myself.

Oceans. Journeys. Lost time.

Land One Sea Two Land Three

Bridge gap bluehole in between two lands. Seaspace lovers on deck. Face to face. Elevated to a state of grace.

Seaman and me. I embark happy as a lark and follow my nose through slices of stone. Wall upon wall. One brick prick I won't miss at all. There are no police on this island. A perfect place to fall from grace.

Moored ashore as the light falls frighteningly hard I find the only bar on the island and begin to drink sink into my holy spirit level time. Double Irish measures increase the pleasure of liquor lines. I stare into my gin pool diving from black bog treacle warmth to fresh white holy gin palaces. In and out. From black to white until my head is clear. Colour rainbows filtered away in black and white decay. I am ready now to find my final heart. My spirit is holy lowly child. I hear myself singing. Poor as I am.

What can I give him
Poor as I am
If I were a shepherd I would give a lamb
If I were a wise man I would do my part
Yet what can I give him
Give my heart.

The mist hovers heavy on this dark Irish night. I can hear the laughing behind me guttural belly lifelaugh of the bigman. I turn and our eyes catch each other. He knows and all he can do is penance when he sees me. He brought wine and flowers and hours of apologies and if only we could undo our selves. Spin backwards to our stardust selves helium high. Truly good. Back to the future. Superman screams of earthturning back back back. You did what you did. Each second you choose your path and he chose his with his hands on my bid to live without dying. Prematurely before I had matured. Like the Hobbit. I need to be 33. I need 3.

Premature. Too early. Untimely. Impulsive. Impetuous. Rash. Incomplete. Undeveloped. Immature. Embryonic.

You are so beautiful . Your smile I am so fucking sorry. Come back to my place. I'll make it up to you.

My beauty and Englishness rose in his fists. He cannot escape his hate and I drink his champagne and slide into his hot tub covering myself with mud caked on my skin to win his heart. I rub myself up against him as he cannot take in me. The English fucking whore. Sooo loud. Drunkencharged Viking energy and we fuck. Me. Mannis, I know the way now. To end the violence. To close the so old testament. An eye for an eye. Rib for rib. Spare part heart. Pumping. I will be cleansed from your sin and when I die. Take my eyes and my flesh and eat me.

He pumps inside out. Fucking away the sins of my ancestors and avenging his family. Stabbing the English cunt. You fucking ENGLISH WHORE! As he comes all over. Inside me. Warm juice to mix the tight clan into something new brighter than stewed genes honeying in pastpain. Paddy potato rain. The sadistic English cunt and the drunken Irish bastard can melt the hatred and violence. I place my deadly dose in his champagne flute with a cute smile and only a few miles to go now.

Poison. A poison in our society. Blight. Bane. Contagion. Canker. Malignancy. Corruption. Pollution.

My potion from the desert. African bulbous bulb from the Desert Prince mixed together with the Berber women who know their place with the strongest face they turn to the world. Now Donal drinks his poisoned flute and no more clan banned session as the music inside him will never come out again. Music that makes our insides worthy of our out. This music I want back. He starts to gurgle and writhe and his big hands contort. No more sculpting the earthy clay. His eyes pop out inside his head and he is dead. So simple. So loving. So kind. I. The body is as heavy as a thousand diver's boots as I pull the plug on his mug and watch the water drain away. The bare fleshy body so weak now all anger and hatred gone and now he is at peace. I cannot eat him here and now so I will chop up his Celtic corpse and follow my plan for the man. Dip him in molted lead dead. Sculpt his outsides. The Iron Man. I will take it back to the desert. My final heart so I can start again.

In his very own sculptors workshop I find his circular saw and start to cut him up into portions for my masterpiece. An arm. A severed head and how I marvel that he is dead.

The sound goes merrygoround blood spurting clown all over me so I put on some goggles to keep the blood from my eyes.

One step two step. One becomes two. Two becomes three and out of the third comes the One as the fourth. There is no light without shadow no wholeness without imperfection. The thorn in the side. Without suffering there is no progress. No ascent.

Ascend. Climb go/move. Mount. Scale. Rise. Levitate. Fly up. Soar. Slope upwards.

I pack limb by bloody stink stenching limb into my rucksack. He wrapped in cloth and covered in love. I climb to the English fortress at the toprock of the hill. The highest point to thrillkill the enemy. The outpost for the persistent blood thirsty English. Made brutality an art. Walking in the steps of my ancestors. The path feels right and familiar. I look over the sea to the next islands and the next I imagine up there on Clare where the castle of the Pirate Queen gleams in light. Shaved bald headed Groyna May who gave out the best blood curdling cry to keep her enemies away. Frozen with fear from this warrior woman who eventually settled down to homemaking cakebaking. Mixing ingredients. The burial ground to do my night's work dipping limbs in lead.

Alchemy transformation. Turning lead to gold.

Figure heartshaped incision around his heartspace. A shape drawn over and over again on dirty schoolbooks back of the class dreaming. I put an arrow across. Always an arrow. Cupids bow slicing through his skin. MP 4 D… I don't even know his name no matter one night stands are all the same. I reach inside for the heart it's shaped nothing like the pictures we drew. Its full and bulbous and alive. Real alien humanity. I wrap it up ready to join the others. The not-so-old father, the begotten Egyptian son and right here right now the most unholy ghost. I set to sculpting the sculptor. A hard day's night's work but my scalpel slishslashes him into shape.

I fuel the fire with treewood to melt the lead in the witch's cauldron. 3 witches.3 wishes. 3 hearts. 3 to be free. I tip my collected wine bottle tops sniffing the lead poison smell. Thousands of bottles of red red wine tops to stop the pain in my hammered brain. Sniff sniff the lead smell quelling me inside. Down below in the fisherman's hut I find the wire to wrap wrap wrap him in. Chicken wire squire ready for the pyre. First the head wired and irondipped. Preserve the feast for the desert alchemy. The fourth. The water of the stone. The resin of the wise. The Arabic Gum. We will be together aqua mercurialis. His blackened eyes stare up at me and I remember the power of his hands throttling my neck and how dare you. I spit at him. I spit. Spit and cry weep wail. Banshee blood and bold ashtears tear me apart. It's so hard to feel stonenothing but I can I can cancan. My final heart broken. I Powerman You you deadlead.

A man passes down below and calls up

What are ye doing there. Burning a body?

He chuckles and walks on.

I sleep among the iron bones until they dry. Feel so lonely now. Need to feel flesh by my side but all I can taste is metallic love and all I want is all of me back.

Early lamb bleating borning yawning morn. I find the fishing boat lapping on the shoreline and an old fishermanface etched in seatime fixed on the sea.

I would like to cross now.

Beware of the swell young lady It will make you sick.

I have to go now.

Yer be mad to do that. You English yer all bloody mad in anycase.

I knock the fisherman with The Iron Man's arm and he falls into his early catch net. Floats out to sea joining his prey as Iron Man does today. I lug his bodyparts in two backbreaking packs. One front. One back and inside out with pain. I slash the rope with my flesh knife and set sail. Man o' war with a sail across my halohead. The sea is calm as my steady arm when I chopped him up into pathetic pieces. Me the captain right or wrong see the islands stone walls disappear.

The calm before the storm.

Inside my stonewalls are crumbling. Me. Ain't that swell.

Swelling my heart feet blistering. Sore. Poor me.

My boat corkscrews through the water and the sculptor and I cross this not so swell swell. The boat is tossed and turned now by the raging rough ageing sea.

Green about the gills.

Queasy Green.

Off colour.

Below par.

Green bile rises and falls as I puke my insides out into the salty sea.

Vomit. Bring up. Regurgitate. Spew up. Spit out.

We're a couple of swells we live in the best hotels….

Singing as the bile rises and falls in my seasick headlegs. Stare at the horizon to balance my sickblasted body. Keep singing Mannis. Everything's gonna be alright.

Nausea. I am...disgusting...sailing...revolting...I am sailing... repelling cross the repugnant sea I am abhorrent crying… forever trying… to be near you… to be free.

Can you hear me….?

Projectile puke my insides out

Can you hear me…?

My man and me. Lovers on our ocean liner. Couldn't be finer. Swell in fact. I stare as hard as Paddington bear at the healing horizon. Can barely see as the sea salt stingrays my myopic eyes and the water lashes my face. Stare and pray for the Ireland to come to view. Catholic guiltcloud of the greenbile Isle. So many deaths. To hell or to Connaught. Burnings and bodies and pray pray pray for all our souls. SOS. Save our souls. The unseen creative dwarf-gods hooded and cloaked manic manikins kept hidden in the treacledark but if you have my vision you can see them. I will. I will So lonely so lonely….Sing Mannis Sing.

Look! There on the seashore little midget fools a foot high. Kinsmen of the unconscious they protect navigation.

NAVIGATION THE VENTURE INTO DARKNESS AND UNCERTAINTY

Small and insignificant but endowed with mighty power. Sing Mannis.

Three have followed where we led

I can see the round-shelled tortoise primitive cold blooded snakelike signs.

But the fourth refused to call

Vomit vortex…Inside-out souless emerald pain

He the rightful seer, he said

Land ho!

His to thank for one and all.

Thank you hope thank you despair thanks for the solution the relief the destination the arrival the journeys end of the rainy bow bow wow owwww….

Thank you LAND.

I drive away as the morning rises cleansing my steamdreams. I drive through this bottle-green beauty Celtic land suffered so much from my ancestors' hands. All is well now his hands are boxed away for the future world to see in museum matt black. Safe museum life. Frozen in time. Harmless. Wrapped up. Boxed up. Mourned. Labelled and understood. Never never in the field of human conflict will that happen again. The road blocks mount as the foot and mouth fears rise. I am questioned about my movements.

Nice day

Everyday you're alive is nice

Have ye come from a farm?

No. I am an artist. I just have my sculpture in the back. Iron man.

Like the Iron Lady.

In a way.

Where are ye taking your man?

Africa where it all began I think. It's a black man with white features. It means we should mix more I think it's the only solution don't you?

I'll be happy to mix with you any of these nights. Yur a fine looking woman.

I move off. Deadset for the airport to export my broken heart. Bodyparts packed in boxes as I slide through customs ducking and dying lying me.

Did you pack the bag yourself?

Oh yes all by myself

You're a sculptor are you?

Yes. A real live artist.

How interesting. Boarding gate 22 G'd luck!

The plane leaves the ground. I so locked blocked inside this tin can. The cloudfluff outside bobs away and I fear these iron birds as much as the Iron man who rattles beneath me. I order a whisky double-triple ripple through my veins so all is right. High as a ten tequila kitenight. Flying through the air I dream of the desert so bold. So wise. So home. Empty quarters where lost smilesouls can restore my inside outcrop. Don't rock the boat. Float through the sky.

I look over the Pyrenees beauty to bring you to your stubborn knees. Please please me. Turbulent life. Trouble and strife. Then the world's worst Concorde burning nightmare. Our Iron plane falls from the sky. I die.

WINDY TALE

I think of the not-so-old man who penned me this tale as life bounces. Ounce after ounce. Announcement away from me.

Inspired by all the winds and particularly the winds blowing in the desert.

The North West Wind was blowing for days and days bringing round white and grey clouds. They were weeping tears of rain but this good wet wind was also showing blue traces in the sky. I was looking at the open window when suddenly the good wind blew a puff in my face. It was bringing a sweet voice and a caress.

The plane dips and falls

They were coming from northern Europe certainly from Ireland at that time. She was in this country. She did not know that this wet and cold wind blowing over her was taking away part of her thoughts.

Edging away this life.

Had she known she probably would have changed her mind and thoughts to show her freedom. But many winds over the world knew her and how to deal with her deep soul and temper.

This is your captain speaking we are fighting against a freak wind. Please. Do not panic.

From the monsoon in Asia, the sea wind in the Persian Gulf, the desert wind in the Omani sands and rocks, the sirocco in North Africa and his brother the simoom. Even their cousins in Europe the mistral; all winds knew her. They had seen her happy, laughing and loving, the Omani wind had wrapped her into his whirl of sentiments, joy and full happiness. Only the big winds knew her sweetness, her intelligence, her temper, and also were worthy of her faithfulness.

We may have to make an emergency landing we cannot continue to fight this wind. Please be patient and above all do not panic.

The sweet voice and the caress to me blown by the north west wind moved my heart. Very big strong winds cannot compel light breezes. This message stayed by me and did not go with the wind.

This is your Captain speaking.

Whiteknuckle fearvoice. He is the captain right or wrong.

We are experiencing turbulence and one of our engines has failed. We will have to make an emergency landing. Do not panic.

From the monsoon in Asia, the sea wind in the Persian Gulf, the desert wind in the Omani sands and rocks, the sirocco in North Africa and his brother the simoom. Even their cousins

in Europe the mistral; all winds knew her. They had seen her happy, laughing and loving, the Omani wind had wrapped her into his whirl of sentiments, joy and full happiness. Only the big winds knew her sweetness, her intelligence, her temper, and also were worthy of her faithfulness.

We may have to make an emergency landing we cannot continue to fight this wind. Please be patient and above all do not panic.

The sweet voice and the caress to me blown by the north west wind moved my heart. Very big strong winds cannot compel light breezes. This message stayed by me and did not go with the wind.

This is your Captain speaking.

Whiteknuckle fearvoice. He is the captain right or wrong.

We are experiencing turbulence and one of our engines has failed. We will have to make an emergency landing. Do not panic.

Panic. Pan. Greek god to whom woodland noises were attributed and whose appearance or unseen presence was held to induce terror.

Pan was there dancing through the aisles half man half goat playing the death pipe. Smoke bellowing into our eyes as we cried. So afraid of our shuffle off this mortal coil and this is not the way the world ends. Not the way the world ends. Not in a bang as we whimper. Scream. Cry. We the passengers do not want to die. The plane dips and dies as our bodies dribble and shake and shit drips from our fearful holes.

Emergency. Emergency. Please go back to your seats.

But Pan never sits as he skips and backflips fear into our floppy fleshsouls. Thrills and chills. Shrilling pipes tuned to kill.

Down into the deepest depths of my gypsy tartheart beating pumping in treble time as we hit the tarmac. Smack and I am knocked out. Boxing bell ringing in my wax-blocked ears.

We are landing at Perpignan airport. Maintain the brace position.

Brace!

Brace!

PERPIGNAN PAIN

All white and dreams bending around time. I am alive. Survival of the shittest. Me. One of the few soul survivors no-one can adam and eve perceive it as the tabloids scream from their sensational remains. Neither The Sun can illuminate nor The Mirror reflect our beautiful world.

MAN O' WAR! Mannis now so alive hardcentred drive.

Man o' war: large Portuguese jelly fish with stinging tentacles.

MAN O' WAR!

Mannis Poor performance artist, was one of 11 survivors of last night's freak accident. She was pulled from the wreckage having sustained minor injuries - a broken rib and leg. The other 141 passengers died on impact as the Ryan Air jet nose dived into the Pyrenees. The cause of the crash is thought to have come from the mistral and sorroco winds tossing the plane into a vortex. Ms Mannis Poor was travelling with her latest art piece The Iron Man and is now recovering in Perpignan hospital. It is thought she was heading for Morocco to exhibit her latest work which has remarkably also been retrieved from the wreckage.

Where is the Iron Man?

It's all right Mannis. Just relax. It's been a long few days.

I see the night nurse and I know I have to find the Iron man and leave. The desert awaits and my heart is still beating. Sole survivor. My rib is broken along with my heart. I have to get to my Iron man.

You'll need your crutches.

Can I see the Iron Man?

Of course. He is safe and sound in the next room.

Is he in pieces?

No he survived without so much as a scrape. Remarkable really.

Broken-legged me. Click click along the white walls. Hospital shining with Midi light that feels right on the skin I am in. She. The nurse. Warm smiling wholly good Nightingale. She. How good she is and how bad is the man of Iron.

All right love I'll wait for you out here.

I love that love. She is Eastender English. The nurse. Salt of the birthearth. I see the gleaming Iron man. Crash survivor. Last man on earth. I take the hospital starch cloth and begin to polish him up. Rub rub. Frottage. So hard on his Iron skin that I begin to see myself reflected in his arms and hands and face. There I am. Unsmiling me. Polished off my man.

Polish: refinement culture elegance of manner

And for one day or maybe three or ten I go to this room and polish and fix my man jigsaw piece him together so he can travel light. Rivets to lockclock him together. Just like that. He stands tall and firm. Polished brutebeauty. I look at myself in his mirror and do not know what I see. I check my ice-box for my three hearts. Red-jelly kidney wobbling magpie hearts. Survivors of an ancient race. The race to begin again. Escape to victory. My leg is deadweight sunk and plastered heavy as heat on a desertday. I must get out to the Desert Prince. Out of here. With my man. I need a plan.

Befriending my nurse nightly. We talk about her life. Troubles and strife she's had in this old life. Divorced from a man who beat the kids and her when drunk as a stinking skunk in a funk. Dunking his biscuits in her tenderly made tea. For better. For worse. Give me my nurse so she can stich bitch me back together. We touch and hug snug as a bug in a jug of women's wine whine whine all the time. I in my prime. Its dinner time. Time for escape from this whitecure scape.

I need to go Ruthie. I need to leave tonight.

You can't love. You need someone to check you out.The police are waiting to talk to you about the disappearance of Gerard Serre. They...

I have to get to my exhibition. I have been working towards it all my life. It means the world to me.

But your parents. They're on their way here...

I spoke with them they can't come now. I'll meet them further south in Tangiers at the exhibition. I need a car. Can you help me please?

Mannis charm to disarm the unknowing world. Champagne eyes that they want to drink clink. I'll love Ruthie's very soulheart till death do us part. Gypsy heart. Secret love. I pass it around. Pass the parcel until the music stops. Her soft flesh arms smell so warm and true. Who would kick his shoe in this face? Running race broken rib against EinSteintime.

Ok Mannis ok.

One more thing I need a rib if you have one spare from the infirmary. A woman's. It is very important.

I can't do that. A body is sacred.

I need it for us for the future.

I sleep in the knowledge that Nurse Ruthie will do my bidding. No kidding. The dawnslant morning striding through newlamb beds. I see the Doctor approaching with news of a new life inside me.

You're pregnant Mannis and the crash may have damaged your baby.

No I am a girl not a woman. No.

No. Not now. Not here. Three hearts is all I need. No life inside must get it out. Must get out. Out. Out.

We'll let you rest. It's probably a shock for you.

Nurse Ruthie returns in the bluedark dead of night with my woman's rib. Alchemy is all and I begin to crawl from my accident bed to where the car is waiting stacked with the Iron Man. I sit beside him. I haul my body inside. Nurse Ruthie drives me across the border to Sunny Spain. Viva España! The wounded girl lies arm in arm with her Iron man contemplating where and when to relieve herself of the seedy seed inside. To have is not to hold. Pro-choice voice Catholic guiltcatch in our Virgin Mary's hand.

SPAIN AND THE ABORTION

Abortion 1 foeticide

2 failure

3 Arrestment of development of any organ esp. a seed or fruit .

4 A person or thing dwarfed or mishapen

Foetus. A possible world that I do not want.

Me. Mannis. The famous foeticide. We drive to the clinic secret world of lost sheep. The Spanish doctors question me and I think of the Dutch Viking abortion boat sailing in the Irish Sea where the doctors have to wear bullet-proof jackets in fear of those snipper wielding lifelovers. A life for a life. Everything deserves to live. ALL! Bacteria. Wisteria. Creeping cancers. Scabies. Crabs. LIVE! Virus on virus. HIV killing cells. Germs. Worms. Piles. All things deserve to exist. The Catholic ladies finger their rosary beads in Spanish churches and heavy kitchens laden down with cross crosses.

We pray to god for all the murderers who have killed his tiny children.

Please return to immaculate conception deception. Life without dirty stinking juices of deathly smells. Give us life without filthyflesh fuck fuck fantasies floating in our beds. Give us innocence and take away this rotten need to feed on our breasts. Boys' toy. The full breasted Man. Old Tiresias' hanging breasts so want want want to return to the soft round wild world of woman. Give us tenderness meek and mild. Save the poor unborn child. Penetration's penance.

Nothing to eat or drink 24 hours before the anaesthetic airfreight flight out of bodily gutbones. Anxious aching starkwhite fear of staying awake and seeing the life sucked out of you. They vacuum it out you know. The Hoover. Hovers over your belly and down to the wombcave lair. Cleans away the unwanted guest. They jest, the amiable anaesthetists, just another day hey!

MURDERER ! says LIFE

LIFE they say

LIFE to the small piglets and bilious bulging balls of breakneck rednecks

LIFE to the 70 year old rapist

LIFE to the fumbling drunken one night stand

LIFE follows if you want to feel inside out

LIFE to everything. All God's creatures. The cancer white cells. The creeping TB. Yellow fever. Typhoid. Dysentry. Malaria. Hep. A B C……si si to the D… D…diseases of nature nature…..

Long Live the verminous black plague. Epic epidemics. And death to

the cure

the relief

the rescue.

I lie on the cold slab of death bed amnesia and stare barebulb eyed at the masked mutiny above me as they take down my waking sails. Voices around me reassuring cottoncloud world of no pain. The crew fix the leak in my hull so I can sail again. Sail without wail. Crazy wanderer in search of the groove. The groove the sailor searches for all his life. Once found, you need never guide or steer the boat again.

The groove.

Blank space. Blanket bliss. The desert sky in pincushioned glitz and glamour hammers home the falling shooting star. It fades fuzz fizzes away. As many stars in the sky as people on earth. One for all of us and thirty ghosts behind each of us.

31 behind me

The unborn child is as is. Un born. Un happy. Un known. Un seen. Un loved. Un kind. Un attached. Un. Un.

Unborn

Born: brought forth by birth as offspring; fig. brought into existence. Started in life. Destined. Innately suited .

Nothing is what it seems. A triangle is better than two points. Opposite mirrorlight blinds the two lovestars. Masks the light spun from their two points. The light from the darklove. The third point. EinSteintime. The star you see from eye to white gem is somewhere else. Bending round space. Lightyears away.

Outside my body has sailed away. Blurred time between the marine maritime ministers of silence and my waking world. Screams of pain in the abortion room. Some feel it more than others. Waking sensation of something past. A blast of space. Opiumhead drifting back into the world.

I am still a girl. Rescued from the abyss. Womanhood suspended.

We can do that now.

Time to go, love.

The 3 hearts are frozen. The Iron Man keeps a watch over them on their way to the burial ground. Nurse Ruthie kisses my hand and I smile wounded bird I. With a broken rib. One-legged murderer in need of a caress. She strokes my head. Soft and gentle.

She is singing and I lie back and dream.

The dream of the lost child.

I left in charge of my niece. It is a real small baby tiny and is getting smaller and smaller and starts slipping from my hands. I have lost it. Her. It. I search under the cushions in the kitchen in the jam pot. I look in my bag. Pieces of paper phone numbers left lipsticks lost keys. I cannot find her. I have lost my new niece. I spy her slipping behind the sofa cushions. She is smaller and smaller. Shrinking and slipping from my hands. Out of reach. Foetus-size peanut child lost in my care. Matchbox girl in my magnifying glasshouse. Finally in heartbeating pump! pump! wee dying hours of the morning I find her. She is there again and feeding from my breast. The feeling as natural as the green grass. As touching as the corner of the eye butterfly flutter by. As primitive as the naked body before the river became glass. Sharp shards shredding our insides from without. The milk of human kindness turned sweet again from my Lady Macbeth dire cruel night.

I awake to frozen hearts.

We stop along the coast. My bones warmer here in sunny Spain. The molten lead man hot to touch. Warmbody reassurance after heartattack dreams. I hold him. Hug him. He is warm but as ever too hard. Morning glory of male desire piercing the woman's soft pillowworld.

Let go.

I must leave. Let go of Nurse Ruthie's apron strings. On the outskirts of Figueres I untie myself from mother love.

Dali's madmuseum monument to hallucination heaven.

Giant golden eggs a grossly fine reminder of the deadly deed.

Thanks for everything. You are one in six billion really. Thanks.

You sure you'll be all right love You quite sure?

Yes we we'll all be all right soon.

I drive my Iron Man and fleshy frozen hearts heading south.

Going somewhere. Somewhere where the sun is shining. Somewhere the weather suits my clothes. Driving too far. Too fast. Always too far.

Faster. The road gets smaller.

Wind in my hair not a care in my sunshine skin.

Powerman.

Losing power throttle choke thrust.

Busted.

The stolen car star stalls and pulls and grinds to a hideous hot halt in Cadaqués. Grabbing my crutches I step outside into the Lorca heat. Limp into a bar full of women playing spin the bottle. Put my hands in my back pocket Bette Davis Style. They offer me drinks and ham from the pig on the bar sliced off bit by bit as I sit oozing pleasure at the salty swine and rioja wine combination. They carouse me into their game lame-hearted me and the bottle spins three times and lands on me. The muscle-mounded headshaved heart pounding goddess takes me in her mouth. She wants me here and now. Drink pumping through our vain veins. Mirror insane body image and I bloodsore from the aborted aching afternoon. Contorted in pleasure as she licks my wounds with so much love feels like heaven above just sent a little angel to my table. I am coming in this Gertude Stein presentness. Wave after bloody wave. Rule Britannia bloodbrain caressed by this strong Spanish tongue. Am harder thanks to your armada of accuracy.

Back in the bar the drinking continues behind the shutters of siesta heat dead time when all is fine and all we can do is wine wine

wine. Women in common. Safe from the prowling purple knights of the streets. Trapped away. A coven of mirrors of understanding and disbelief. The other mother. I drink until I can think and am kissed all over. My white cliffs of Dover. Santamaria. Wished the best goodbye from the pretty piglets in the sty. Hasta luego.

I check The Iron Man and see my drink sparkle shining eyes in his shiny chest. After woman I want man. Right or wrong. I clutch the steering wheel and feel my way into the hot chorizo charm of this Spanish night. Heading for Lorca country on the way to my very own Blood Wedding. Kissed all over feel the x x x crosses on my body. Head in rags….. Tarra gonna a a a long distance. I feel a brute shooting pain in my broken bone leg. I drive one footed automatic for the people. Plastered up half of me. Soon to be free.

BARSOLONELY

A solo visit to see Sagrada Famiglia. That endless labour of love erecting the genius vision. Stretching up from the Barssolonely city to breath giraffe air. The giraffeheart must beat strong enough to reach the top of the neck and reach the braintower. Me. Mannis. Go visiting. Wandering through the ground floor ruins of this dancing building and I see an ancient man rising from the rubble with a craggy chorizo-face.

He offers me a private tour.

I give you special tour inside and outside.

I have access to private places.

This building is like us...joven and viejo.

He laughs with the drag of history at the curious cathedral uniting old and young hopes. We walk up narrow steps narrowing our safety and reach a small balcony view just room enough for two and his arms are either side of my waist looking for this corner to be forever England. My short skirt lifted to feel his hard saucisson rubbing against me. Frottage frenzy in Spain takes me back to the French train and we'll always have Paris. His chorizo breath asks for a kiss. His face is as old as Europe. Traintracks running deep into the fleshy tissue. I turn. The only way is up. I look down to the minute midgets far away on the Catalan ground. Spin round and he has me armtrapped. Lips push on mine and I duck and fly to his side. Race. Me. Down the steps. I run and he pants behind but he is no match for my strong leg. One-legged angel. I can still fly. He runs out of breath lungs weakened by coolwhite Ducados tar…

Ta! Ta! hasta luego!

The old man coughing up blood in his ivory tower denied the cream dream flesh of youth. Long in the tooth but human. Rumplestiltskin yearning for Rapunzel. He would do anything to pump again.

He climbs this tower every night.

Alone.

And every night.

He stands at the very top and looks down over the dancing city.

ON THE ROAD TO TANGIERS

Destination Tangiers. Full of queers and tears of the aching arses raped for leisure pleasure. Relax with a cocktail to the sound of the young boys' wail. No need for camels here plenty of young blood. A perfect place to show off my beauty. My Iron Man. Though the hole is blocked to the cock. Inside out he'll never be a man again. Never make music. Never steal my honeysmile.

EXHIBIT HIM.

Clothe and derobe him. Shame and name him. Revenge is sweet. Erect the Iron Man. Foot and legs and stomach and torso. Head placed on top. Screwed in place. White Celtman withering in a black face. Space race time beams down on us.

I drive until I need to drink. Drive myself to drink. Thinking of my hard as nails Iron Man and what I will do now I have him. I wander from bar to bar. Bra to bra falling on hot stone floors. Lines of white powder searing up my nose to expose this need need kneading of human flesh miles and miles of sunshine sublime heattreat thawing my wet dampboned weathered body. I think. I can. Weather the storm. I stop to thinkdrink in a small town. Jerez. Full of sherry. The syrup nectar for piddled middle England.

Like a drink?

Well it's a bit early

Oh go on ! Mums the word

Sh! Sh! Maybe just a sherry then

Jerez . Slurred into sherrez. Slurred JJs into shugar shweet sherry silverspooned surburban mouths.

A far cry from its origins.

Here and Now in Sweet Sherry Spain. Old and young sit and sip in small dollcups in subterranean bars as the street steams hot as a baking potato inside its skin. I always eat the skin it's good for you. I sip swig cup after cup. I walk along the baking boiled-egg streets. Silent stench rising from the hysterical gutters. Gutless wonder wandering alone.

I never knew sherry was so good. I fumble in Spanish.

No say

just an old aunts drink.Tanta.

Sweat drips drains from my sherrybody.

Sherry cherie...cherry.

Legless.

Knitted Auntie. Sweetstained glass Christmas windows and church hymns. Decanter bottled with mysterious disappearing nectar necked as she sat next to her husbland. Must go sherry sh… shopping to buy some clothes for him. Such a fat neck it is hard to find a suit to suit him. What colour would he like? Red White and… or Blue maybe…

Can I help?

Yes I'm looking for a suit for my husband. He is a big man... granda si si

The shop assistant has dark gypsyskin. Olive deep and his piercing eyes break through me. He steadies me as I clutch my crutches.

Will you meet me later we can talk drink eat?

How kind to ask a cripple.

I am on a journey. My man is travelling with me.

Okay we find him a suit.

And Luis, the danger pumping from his dark Spanish eyes,

takes me through an array of men's sizes. All shapes and colours. Size matters. Must fit like a glove. Cool conditioned respite on this hot afternoon. He shuts the shutters as I mutter sherry blurred and buried in desire's pyre. Everything is painted black as I feel his body against mine. Smell of strong aftershave waves shot through my skin. He kisses me hard fullforce. Morse code flash warning lights through the dark blinds. I am blind. Love is blind. I am Love. Blinding Love.

SaulPaul forgiven.

And after woman comes man. Man.

Oh Man!

Su nombre?

Man…Man…

Qué?

Man….

And he slides down my chest as the bell rings.

Leave it.

He is licking my thighs inside. Bloated flies fizz in my eyes. Thighs and then just the tip outside to make the inside rise dream topping high. Needing inside now screaming inside for him to fill fill fill me up.

GOD.

He undoes his jeans fit to burst and I can feel all of him. Both full fruited ripe. And this is the way the world ends and begins. In a bang. YES. In a bang. YEEES INSIDE not out. In a bang GOOOOOOOODDDDDDDDDDD.

God is love.

So GOOOOOOOOOOD

as we whimper.

Breathless

Deathless

Me

I buy the biggest suit in the shop and leave with a smile .

Driving Time. Moving but still. The plastic seats burn my legs. Lorca landscape land of blistering women watching their sons grow into violent men. Watching and pressing heat spray hissing ironing starch white shirts. I need to sleep sleep and dress my man for dinner. I keep on driving until I can no longer feel or think just road and light and press my foot down to erase the pain and heart rain. No regrets. This must be done and I am the chosen one. I stop on an empty road and feel the mooncold light call me. It is so full it hurts and the Lorcawoman in me wants to come alive and spurt naked blood across the star lucky sky. I cry for myself. Lost in mud. Brain gone numb. Must go back.

To the Desert Prince

Who will always be waiting

Unconditional dove

HONEYMOON IN MOJACAR

Love is a many splendored thing!

I reach Mojacar. A towering inferno of blatant bold beauty. A white crown of purity on the hill overlooking the sea. I circle and weave myself up the dusty trail. Donkey tired. Heart beating to burst. I see a pensión for lovers. I enter and am shown the most beautiful room I have ever imagined. *Not* plush rich beauty but earthful whole and right. The lady of *the* house is wise and deep.

It's so beautiful.

We only allow people to stay two nights otherwise no one would ever leave. People. Couples come in fighting and leave over the moon honeymoon syrup sweet to each other.

It's magical!

Later sitting on the balcony drinking thimbles of fino I hear Noël Coward scratching record singing up to me. I start to dress my man. Dress for a feast by the shoreline. I iron his white shirt Lorca lostlove. As I look at the starchwhite collar blots of blood appear clear as a redlight late traffic light.

Blood.

Arms up!

Blood. It's the heat. Out damned spot out I say.

Arms up!

But they don't move. I put on his trousers. Zip up his flies.

Suited and booted.

My nose is bleeding.

I tie his bow tie and see an aluminous green butterfly dead in his eyes and crickets croon cracking my insides out.

Let's go out darling. It would be a shame to stay in on a night like this.

Lugging the Iron Man down the donkey trail our hobeyloon rail.I mean honeymoon tale.

We sit by the shore and I lay out a chequered picnic cloth.

The moment of beauty romantic love. Aching artfelt anticipation of the food and love to come.

Aperitif sexpectations saliva.

I take my Iron Man to the sea. Tapas for two.

Me and you.

Silhouetted in lieu of the things to come.

Me and you.

We sit starring at the ocean and I lay out the food.

Fish Olives Patatas Octopus Manchego Chorizo

My favourite.

Not to forget the deep bloodwedding feelfine wine. Bread and wine. Drink.

Would you like a drink?

No reply. Not very talkative this man of mine. Lost his heart like Dorothy's rusty old tin man. I take out the olive oil. Extra virgin. Extra.

Virgin snow/territory; pure, immaculate, unblemished,
spotless, stainless, unused, untouched, untainted, unspoilt,
untarnished,unadulterated.

More than pure enough to feed the Iron Man's aching joints. I put it on his mouth to loosen those lips that used to spout sputter guttural sounds.

The oil drips stunning down his chin and slides as the fullfat orange Moon sinks solo heavy into the sea.

He and Me

A lovely place for a honeymoon

All right sweet honeysugar pie?

No reply

I eat fish after fish delicious white anchovies slither down inside me and I lay back and make love licking him all over. The Sculptor. Every crack and crevice of his strongbow body. I can feel him shiver and shake what a good lover I make.

I roll over post coital postmodern posted him to heaven.

Stars we are.

Thinking.

Clever constellations consistently pushing out bowel beauty light. No stella cityconstipation here. I strip off and swim in the darknight water lit by generations of love. Little glitter lights all over my beautiful body. My heavy wounded leg is numb. I swim athletic arches of power back and forth under my moon.

Come on in the waters lovely.

He cannot swim obtain the unobtainable. His iron fleece must tarnish to goldrust. Tis rust alone that gives the coin its worth. My buried treasure.

Dance Minaloushe dance

Turn black to gold.

I lay on the sandshore naked as the sandblown glass neath me and feel the sea reach my insides then out in and out and the frothfull foam gathers inside me until I come from here to kingdom come in a scream a cry an or gas mmmm.

Orgasmspasmchasm

Home to the honeymoon suite and when sleep comes the drink sinks me into oblivion. My favourite kind of dreaming is none.

Pack up the Iron Man in strawbox crates and smile, smile, smile. Farewell Piccadilly Farewell Leicester Square…His head cut from his body dissected arms in one box legs in another and the three hearts in another. Not forgetting Nurse Ruthie's rib.

All packed?

Says the hostess with the mostest.

Yes Thank you we…I had a lovely time.

You must come back.

Yes but right now I must go forward.

I understand.

TO ALGECIRAS

We set off. Iron Man and I. Honeymoon sated. Belated lovers. The day heats and smokesneaks up on us. Leaving the treetrunk earth. Bullfighting me flashing my redheart flag. Tempting the blind bullyman. Myopic hot madras and his mojo. One flick. Toreador me. Soon to be free to eat the bullmeat sold outside my soulstadium. Arrows point me in the right direction. South down to the hottest core.

Just the two of us.

We can make it if we try.

You and I.

Corazón Cruiser. I put my hand on his hot limbs and only 100 straight miles to go before we cross the straightrocks of Gibraltar. The cross Celtic sculptor. Heavy cross Catholics carrying the world on their shoulders and the children on their knees. Teaching them God is Love. Stroking them into the fold.

It's a secret.

The Lord is My Shepherd. I shall not want want want you my sweet innocent child.

Passing houses on hills laden down with Martyr Mary and gentle Jesus Meek and Mild.

Immaculate conception. Desire's Deception.

The only pure man alive. Apart from the innocent child.

Crucify your desires. Pull apart your flesh and nail it to the criss cross.

Stigmata

Feeling small as the mountains bawl their primal scream.

See the mountains kiss high heaven

And the waves clasp one another

I stroke my hot metal man.

No sister flower would be forgiven

If it disdained its brother

His skin burns mine

And the sunlight clasps the earth

And the moonbeams kiss the sea

I turn and kiss his cheek.

Blistered lips.

What is all this sweet work worth

If thou kiss not me?

I leave Nurse Ruthie's car at the port. Algeciras drunks and pimps and prostitutes. I drink bellybeer and slither anchovies to build my strength to lug the iron mug on my back.

Uno ticket Tangiers.

Regreso?

No, solo.

SOLO.

Past the cars and my breakneck back is stacked high with my toadload. African mountain woman from the very first six. Clutching crutches. Hands numb. One Step. One crutch. One Breath. One Love. I can see the boat to float me away from here.The Black Swan.

Embarkment.

AFRICA beckons. La Linea. The Line. Thin blue sea. Dividing me and me. The sea to take me back inside myself. Beside myself with hope as I fly forward backwards against the thermal current. The migrant birds flit float over my bedhead. Angels from Africa scarring my skyeye. Headturning beauties leaving me. Flying to Gibraltar with the warm air streaming through their wings. Joining those cheeky English Monkeys on rocksolid angled time.

In between the past and the future. I am present.

Crisscrossing EinStein time.

One Shot.

One Time.

Downing my Anglo Stein.

THE CROSSING OVER

Sailing away from Europe. Your rope. Past noose loosening around my neck as I hit the deck. Iron Man and Mannis me. Smiling beguiling soon to be free. Spain disappears with its sultry drip drip inside me. I stare at the sea. Another crossing. Far further this time. Wave adieu to Europe. Old haggard bloodstained continent. The ancient old world webbed in the Viking past politics of the heavy rope. Celt belt loosening around my neck. Hit me with your belt. Squeeze me till I'm Celt. Europa Hot with rage when clan we turn the page?

Spain smelling itch to stay but come what may I must leave you. For good?

Are you going for good?

Goody good bye but I won't forget you until the end of time. All the good times we spent. Laughing childhood me playing at sea lost on the island when the tide came out. Runaway brothers and sisters. Parents sweet work and my sister carried me wading through the deep water back to shore where the Mum and the Dad were waiting to take us home and Elvis sang that there is nothing quite as pretty as Mary in the morning and I wet my bed but the man the big man he was there there there. Wet through me dried by the wind love blown from the mother's lips the mother of all cities built on peace and then comes the violence the hate and the pain as I turn burn my head to Africa where it all did or did not begin. My child within hanging behind can't ketchup hanging by yourrope but must grow up go up towards the future. Extinguish me. Catherine Wheel firework past past as we past another boat waving waving going backwards as I speed forwards towards Einstein time and this is the way the world is is is here now water and waves and turn your back on home coz there is no place like no place like. The waves know how to say hello then wave goodbye.

The desert hot pen drops. I can no longer remember. Must get stronger.

Horizon gazing I remember another journey on a different boat on the Irish sea. The boat that brought him back to me. The Big French Prince. He came with no language but more than enough love to fix the car, stoke the fires, keep us warm. Inside me with his full Gallic loving-feasts to fill me to the brim with love. The Frenchman and I. Oyster close like the Beat poets understood bestowing our pearls carelessly. We are together in the shell as crystalline as snow. He cut the sea anemones for me to eat as the Sligo sea washed over he and me. And remember whatever we lose like a you or a me it's always ourselves we find at the sea. His huge laugh echoes across the blue grey light of the sea. We melt into newer forms as the stars gently spin around our heads.

Will you marry me? He said.

Who was I?

I was playing Maud Gonne no Lady Macbeth, or the Queen. My hair was golden, red or black. But I remember the Big Prince with strong kind hands and a knife in his back pocket. He stopped speaking for five years. He dreamt he had wings and he flew so much that his arms hurt. I remember him. That man was so good. In his dreams he carries the children across the river. He follows a dog as he flies and sometimes he has to repair the dog. As he had to repair me. I see him sitting sewing my dress by the tinkling trickling river. The

Shannon river a tributary tribute to his open heart and I lost myself. Slowly delicately with the slightest of touch he stitches in and out the white silk dress that the revolutionary Maud was wearing. I was wearing. Maud was wearing. Sweet prince. The dress was torn from the bracken. Stichbitch me hurt that Big Prince. We could have been fine if they had not got to me first. If I had another chance to rewind the Catherine Wheel past but once lit it just keeps on spinning. My Big Prince. Good night sweet Prince and flights of angels sing thee to thy rest.

Maud believed in re-incarnation so much so she had sex on the grave of her poor dead baby George. Her baby who she left in Paris while she tried to stop the hate and the pain of the brutal Brits who pulled down the poor Bog peoples' huts and houses but Maud stood tall in the Lough land flaming ravenous red hair towering over the wee Celts. She carried a gun in her boot.

Where is my child....?

Did I leave it in Paris? I cradle the playbaby. It is just a sheet that falls and dies. Maud's baby. That was the play. The play.

Where is my baby?

I am a girl not a woman. I did not conceive concede to this life full of heat and hate.

The instant of ecstasy. Penetrations penance. One instant of ecstasy weighs heavier than a whole life time. I remember a child but I am a girl not a woman. They all had to go. The guilt seeds were all shed so why in my bedhead do I hear you call to me in this vast desert sheltering sky. Bowling me over singing and laughing. Roaring at me across time.

Moooootheeeerrrrrrrrrr!

And the ship moves forward.
AND THE CLOCK GOES BACKWARDS…
But. I will love
you
until
the end of time.
And the boat sails on through this picture yourself world.

TANGERINE SKIES

Tangerine sun splits my eyes as we sail into port hustled to spend 2! 2! 2! dirhams on freshly-squeezed oranges juiced at the speed of light. Tangiers the mongrel city cross breed world-weary port welcoming world weary me. Phoenicians Romans Visigoths Arabs Portuguese British and Spaniards. The smugglers money-launderers gunrunners MY FUCKING AUNTIE... prostitutes and pimps all flourished in this Sodom and there's no tomorra Gommorah. Sodomy. Bigamy. Cannibalism. Tangier once Tingis where Hercules slew the giant Antaeus and fucked his widow Tinga without a tinge of guilt spilt. My sins are welcome here. Almost natural. Tangiers... the international zone.

If you see her say hello she might be in Tangiers.

One step on to this African land. The time is lunar lunacy. 1423. Medieval me.

Squinting on my rocking horse licking the tangerine sky. Blood on my sandals.

The Desert Prince is standing there on the shoreline through the smog and smoke and smell of donkey skins on route to the tanneries. Tanneries where the young boys sweat away skinning the softgoats leatherskin used to bind Her Majesty's books. Comforting hands on a book. A whole new world inside that is yours. Someone always has to die for your pleasure. For Her Majesty's secret pleasure, royal books spawned from goat's heads and rotting skin. Ismail is there smiling African Prince to take me to the Promised Land. He understands. Takes my head in his hands.

You are beautiful.

He guides me through the city batting off the hustlers with a glint of an eye. Eyelash flick whips away the unwanted grabbing hands. A slight move and they know. Mannis me blonde goddess of light in the blackheaded sea. He walks ten paces ahead and carries my packages on his back. We cannot be seen together. The African Arab boy with a whitebreasted wested woman. Girl. Still a girl. The men are terrified of *fitna.* The epitome of the uncontrollable dangers of sexuality and its rampant disruptive potential. As we all know one thing leads to another and *fitna* leads to *zina;* Illicit copulation! So run from Aisha Kandisha. A repugnant female demon lying in wait behind every dark corner, lusting in wait in each shadowy alleyway. Libidinous breasts and lips assaulting men in the streets. Inducing them to fuck. Penetrate their bodies and stay with them forever..

Drip dripping tales of womannotsokind.

Masochistic Moroccan police want to stamp out false guiding. Arrest the young boybeauties who play with each other like tumbling krazylazy cubs or kittens. Good crazy. The police want to spoil them soil them. Would torture my bluesky desert Prince. Torture him cut his arms for the crime of guiding. It's right up there with murder and theft and sodomy.

Sod em. I say.

A faux guide leading us astray. Unofficial. Unauthorized. Unsanctioned wildcat. No badge. No papers. No bullshit. My wildcat licks my wounds. Without him I am finished. Endgame. Over the cliff Thelma and Louise style. And woman needs man and man must have his mate that no one can deny. A kiss is just a kiss.

I show Jimi Hendrix round last year.

Just creative myth-makers.

These young boys. Free as flamingo birds swooping down to drink from the spied oasis.

Guiding. It's a very serious crime. Ain't that the truth.

These boys risking raw bones to take some money to their families.

My one is lucky he never gets caught.

They have big hearts and giddy golden eyes in search of the treasures inside Aladdin's cave. These Aladdin boys at their peak of faith. Honest knaves.

We head for villa.

Ismail has a friend here. They are all friends or cousins or uncles. Until crossed. We duck into an alleyway and I cover my legs from the leering red eyed Majoun munchers. A sticky pasty ball of paranoia turning your insides out. The heat is on and I have made it this far just following his worldly African head. Small squeezed curls of comfort not loose western hair but tight sure right on a Berber night.

Sunglass armour block these windows to my soul. To ward off the evil eye. For your eyes only. Once in these men never get out. They crawl inside your blue eyes and leave a silt trail slimed into your intestines. Beware of the glare the power of the eyes. Cavernous blue holes that cascade waterfall fools into your insides and never let them out. Beware the glare.

Soon. I spot posters everywhere.

THE IRON MAN

Controversial performance art exhibition by Mannis Poor
Musée d'Art Contemporain
Rue d'Angleterre Tangiers

Here in the desert we are waiting for the Spring. Pink Flamingo flock preparing for the birth and the burial of the 3 Hearts. We kiss for as long as a walk through the Sahara. Lying here his tongue so long snaking inside me and here there is only outside. Blank space emptyheaded Me. And I am losing the guiding star EinSteintime to tell you my story and we are beginning and ending in the desertsun the summer the present continuous Steintime. And I am coming to you in sickness.....

I follow my African trueguide as he ducks and dives through alleyways. I feel alive. No longer alone someone to carry the stone burden. We reach the door of the villa. Plainstone marks the outside but the gems await inside of this Morrocan den. The door is marked with a Hand of Fatima to protect us from evil spirits. The private interior for women.

Domestic quarters for women. Harem.

Rooted words ***harem***. Literally meaning *the sacred area* if trod upon becomes haram. Dirtied. Crossed. If shown too much flesh. Skinfuls. Haram. Translates to us as sinful. The door to the secret garden opens and a fountain appears the music sprinkletinkles your senses. The sound of music.

Musical tuneful melodic harmonious mellifluous sweet-sounding dulcet euphonious.

Antonym HARSH DISCORDANT GRATING

The birdsong is free sweeping swooping across fields and cities they sing little feathered lives. The good ones but the magpies have no song nor the vultures or ravens that tear apart the rundown cat on the country road. Only her fur coat left plastered to the road where car after car accelerates over her burial ground. Ugly toads.

The Desert Prince guides me to a sun-warmed cushioned chair.

Stay there. You relax. You sit and you think. I make tea.

Mint tea the smell of mint printed on my pheromone mindpage that sits smelling in your head right next to your long term memory brain slot. One sniff and you get the lot. The whole catherine wheel spinning past pictures coming rewind back to your fast forward life.

Cut grass blasts you back to sports winning day. Making hay. Aftershave crave the Daddy protection of manly odour strength. Suncream sends you skiing schooltrip down the slopes. Burnt faced white skisuit turned red from the first period piece trying to make me a woman. Coffee in the morning a lover clattering the cups. A taste of things to come. You can fall in love with a smell. Garlic in the kitchen and onions in my eyes.

Sizzling bacon sausage fingers.My midnight feasts in the desert.

Memory's Empty Quarter

by the sea

on the island

you and me.

The tanneries smell of hell. Stench foul smell reek mephitis noisomeness whiffniff pong.

But here heaven is a place on earth. A haremhaven.

Fruit trees languishing under laurels and cypress shade.

Just jasmine rose and geranium scent sent from heaven which

surely is on earth.

You must sleep and rest. Tomorrow is big day. Your performance.

He tucks me in a big soft African blanket with wild animal prints all over. Sleeping in the jungle but safe as houses. He strokes my forehead so hard and scarred and large. My first scar when my Daddy held out his arms to cuddle me bearhug Father there there there. He sitting in a rocking chair and I running faster to him there and the wooden arm sticking out from the threadbare chair. Smack crack split my egghead. Blood everywhere. He sweeps me up into the car to Mayday.

Aidez-moi! Aidez-moi!

Mayday hospital where I lie while doctors stitch my head a stitch in time.

What a brave boy!

She's a girl says my Dad.

And he takes me home hugging me so tight and I love him with all my might and whatever happened to all the good men Fathers in heaven?

Ismail strokes my scar bar after bar head.

I succumb to the motherly caress and think of my mother's soft flower dress in our hazy sunshine garden and I never wanted to stop smelling her dresses they smelt of roses and jasmine and violets and love. All the colours were there alchemy's answer turning me into gold. Little Mannis bold as brass but showered in gold. Stolen gold looted from my once shiny skin.

Sweet dreams with many colours

So he knows yes he knows. It is in silence that we know each other. Desert silence soon. Sun's shelter after my coming storm.

PERFORMANCE

The Cast

Mannis as Woman 1

The Iron Man as The Iron Man

The characters are locked in a cage like you would see in a circus. The Iron Man is on a little platform similar to the ones elephants are put on to perform tricks. Like standing on one leg. Woman 1 has a whip and is the Ringmaster.

Woman 1 dressed in a suit and tie and The Iron Man in full veiled hijab black bedecked from head to toe and a beak mask for his face.

Discordant.

Those eagle style masks you see in the Persian Gulf and on a sunny afternoon in Hyde Park. The arabic music blares out from the tinny mini sound system.

Grating.

Mannis starts to dance undressing the Iron mummified man. She caresses him from head to toe and starts to feel his thickprick. There is a bucket of water to one side and she starts to wash her face.

Haram Haram

Sinful sinful

She begins to wash his body wash and polish she wipes his arse and tells him everything is going to be alright. His prick is splendid big enough.

Try before buy! She screams in Arabic.

Woman 1 begins to loosen her tie and take off her white man's shirt. We see her full ample breast. She climbs on the back of the Iron Man and tries to breast feed him.

Harem!

The crowd gathered begin to throw things at the performer nuts mainly that hit and bounce off the bars. They are appalled but cannot leave transfixed and rooted to the spot. One man calls security.

HARSH

The music changes to farewell adieu to you and you and you sound of music escape as Mannis bids the wide-eyed crowd goodnight. Ismail grabs the Iron man and they exit out the back of the cage where Ismail has a cousin getaway car foot on the breakmate ready to barfburn his tyres out of there. They run for their lives. Scarper!

Artful exit.

Police sirens are heard as we drive through the Socco Chico sleazy slum up into the Kasbah which we rock. Spilling ceramic colours and leather luxury across the streets. James Bond style. The car halts at The Gate of Rest. A dead end turn and I can see Spain basking in its limelight. The driver backfires crashing into the police and speeds back through the Medina. Stoned Interzone notoriously near Paradise on Earth. The Garden of the Hesperides. Not near enough as the smoke fumes blacken my face and Ismail screams to his cousin.

Zid! Zid!

We make it out of Tangiers. Just. And the silence of the African night is music to my ears.

FEZ JUST LIKE THAT!

Fez the heated heart of Morocco we arrive just like that to purchase Omani treasure chests lying deep in the bazaar. Three fat hard silvergold chests to bury my bruised breasts. Dig deep in my chest for the stolengems of the bygone days. I carry my healthy hearts. 3 hearts a rib and an Iron Man.The Desert Prince and I in search of the burial ground. Ground the hearts to bring me back to earth. Stolensmile childlike I.

Fez formed from axe. A golden axe unearthed in the birth of Fez. Chopped up. Just like that. Cooper heart stopping comedy. Laugh until he died. And I am beginning and ending in the summer. The comedy season. In EinSteintime. I am laughing galaxy gaffaws shooting across the sky. Roaring storms of laughter blowing in the wind. The Sirroco. The Mistral. Laughing all the way to the banks of the river Nile. Smile. Laugh I nearly went to Africa. Sub-Saharan where millions are dying in the present continuous not laughing but crying of AIDS. Sex has always killed.Van Gogh.Baudelaire. De Sade.Syphilitic madmen driven inside out by the old in-out. The death blow inside each other and no escape from the wombtomb. Bury my cherry hearts. We wind and grind through the narrow labyrinth of bursting burping smells covered in pipeshaft light. Crisscrossing through bamboo roofslats.

Tu aimes Fez?

Oui.

Ismail hands me a mint sprig to take away the thrusting death perfume in the tanneries where the goats' swill swirls and the visitors throw up in the door way. Mint seasoning hint. Heaven more than a glint away from the Horror the Horror of the terror tanneries. Chromium salts sulphuric acids animal fats and brains. Put the monkey in the hole in the middle. Take a golden Fez axe and slice off the top of the head. Pick up your silver spoon and eat the brains. A Chinese delicacy. Dogs too and here cats if you're not careful. Sacred cows in the west. Oral satisfaction. Flesh for flesh an eye for an eye. Turn hell hound turn the other cheek. Gentle Jesus meek and mild where is your fighting force? Impotent wanderer not-so-old thorn-crowned man.

The heat.

The horror.

Perhaps If I had kept the skin I could have made a coat of mannotsokind.

Oui J'aime bien.

Vraiment?

Oui Oui mais je veux faire pee pee.

I enter a back door which becomes another door and through another. Blind alleyway dens full of bones unburied and heaps of pulping putrid matter.

What's the matter lady?

Twist and turn and dust thick.

Stench wrenching my heart back back before the bad set in. Maggot rotting in my core and rotting fruits and blood scrapped bones and cats with devil faces and white eyes staring inside me and there is no exit no out

then

just like that

hocus pocus harum scarum abracadabra allakazam!

The genie from the lamp.

There is an end. A door. I open it and there a banquet feast at the end of the tunnel.

Light out of black. Men in white welcome me like I was the Princess of the world. So kind. So open.

Come in little girl.

Trust Me. Trust me.

In here and I do I do.

And there is the golden loo hole in the ground. A la Turque a cordon bleu dish. Nose of Turk and liver of Jew. No way out of Fez des res. Deeper we go through the helterskelter lanes. In search of the chests to bury deep my sins so they no longer will be visiting. Carnage calm. The smell of the crowds the roar of the greasepaint. All eyes on me. At each and every corner they are waiting.

Barek! Look out!

The mule driver cries as they knock you off your feet.

The city is crumbling.

Barek!

Could fall down any minute. The world could stop turning,

Barek!

The sun could go out.

Decrepitude: cracked falling to pieces the art of falling apart.

DECAY: rot, go bad, putrefy, spoil, perish, corrode.

Degenerate: ebb, dwindle, crumble, disintegrate, wither, atrophy, moulder.

We enter a cave of jewels fool's gold diamonds and rubies and sapphire and steel steal my stolen heart. A chest for a chest. An eye for an eye. A tooth for a tooth. A heart for a heart. 3 Witches. 3

hearts.3 wishes.

Blaspheming liver of jew
Gall of goat and slip of yew
For a charm of powerful trouble
Fire burn and cauldron bubble
Cool it with a baboon's blood
Then the charm is firm and good
Rib of birthdead babebone
Ditch-delivered by a nurse alone
Heart of Arab
Blackcroaked scarub
Heart of green
Humpbacked lean
Heart of wealth
Watery health
From sweet to obscene
Bubble hell broth
To thy Queen
From black to gold
Fortunes told
Old Iron man
GOLDEN CHEST AXE
In the pan
Just like that.

Very good this chest coming to you just 1000 Dirhams.

EinSteintime. I walk around the cave of rich stitched up prices but what price to pay to bury the Catherine Wheel past.

The past is priceless.

In search of a pattern. Moroccan Art is all patterns not a moving flesh and blood spirit. Living things are forbidden to be forged into art. Do not prostitute them here. Haram. Geometry only. Generous and safe. Living things in Art are Pagan decadent. NOT ALLOWED!

But my Iron Man is only living on the inside soon to be buried alive. Outside. In the desert sands. My rolled gold comfort blanket bliss. One grain of sand for every universe out there. Our blue planet a drop in the ocean. Heart aches.

Alchemy answer my call.

You choose you like?

Ismail helps me pick out my treasures and they are carried to the waiting car. A limousine hired for the burial queen. Blacked out windows. The car arranged by Charlie Brown. A true guide with a smile as tight as a Halloween cut pumpkin. If Charlie Brown's happy everybody happy.

Charlie Brown No Drinking! Charlie Brown Happy! Everybody Happy!

And Charlie takes us to his family home deep in the depths of Fez. We sit squashed tomatoes and stew in this biblical world as Southfork family life plays on in the background. Worlds apart. We feast on fish tajine shared and eaten from one bowl. Bread for a spoon. Heads down smiling. No individual JR portion here. Glossy soap slippery serial dreams and if abortion is murder well hell I'm a serial killer.

Men and women cousins sons daughters husbands wives tied together like the network of stars worldwide spiders web and I a fly caught for a while. My ties broken family lost me. In my dark killing fields mind. No one understands the mistake of too much love.

I thank the family and go. Sweat is dripping cold down my burial back. My head spinning mint tea too many Morrocan whisky. I need the real thing and sure nuff the limo slides a bar in front of my mirage-worn eyes. Dallas-style.

Nothing is what it seems and no one exists alone we must love one another and die.

Ismail holds me close to him and he smells of sweetest Africa of life before my strife began. He cares my baby for me not for clothes just for me not for high class places. His tongue just for me slides inside and out of mine in the limousine. Hot Sahara breath thawing my steelysore heart. Touches tender my skin. Kissing me all over wrapped up in love. Whispering sweet everything into my ear. Promises of more and more loving smoothskinned African love for me to start again. It's a nice day for a blood wedding. A nice day to start again.

DEVIL IN DISGUISE

To reach the Sahara and stay hidden I must never speak. I move with my cloak of secrecy through secluded walled courtyards and hidden door-ways painted luminous blue. Blue is the colour to ward off evil. Like my eyes but still it tries to sneak in. This evil. Women clad in *burkas* and *djellabaclad* men together with vendors of amulets and potions. Concoctions that are all guaranteed to ward off the evil eye.

On the running road to Casablanca to hideout for a day or two. Disguise myself. Rest my rotten leg and broken rib. Wanted Me. Finally wanted by them. Under suspicion but not the usual suspect. We stop on the long dry desert road in a small Baghdad Café to do some magic. Henna dye my hair to blend inside the black headsea. Dyed once before. Was it blond for the Viking Queen or red for flaming Maud or Black for Lady Macwitch? Life is not a rehearsal but with no rehearsal how could I have carried out the plan. They are dead and gone lady. The kind Irish hairdresser with skin that was warm and weather torn. She needed no facial facade. Not lipstick powder nor paint just because some men prefer your lips red not as God meant but as he intended. Deep rich voice Celtic accent made me hang my shamed English head. Strangled, raped and knifed.

Your hair is very fine. Are you sure you want to dye it so dark.

Yes it's for a part.

O you're an actress then. How fascinating

Yes. I'm playing Maud Gonne. She was an extraordinary woman. It filled me with such power and pride to play such a great lady and in London some Irish people bowed to me and kissed my hands.

You must have been very good.

I looked them in the eye. I wanted to make amends.

What part am I playing? Now.

Cover myself in full hijab. Fill myself top to toe with the direst cruelty. Unsex me here. From blonde to red to black. Turning gold into metal. An alchemist's nightmare. Reverse myself. Turning me inside out.

They'll never find you. You are with me now. Always.

All ways.

He will screw his courage to the sticky place and he will not fail. My hands are black with diedye and yet I shame to wear a heart so white. I look in the mirror and I see a new me. Black-blue eyed like a bruise. Make up to bronze me and no-one would know me. Not even me. Witchlike now. Not a white one but a black.

Rib of birthdead babebone
Ditch-delivered by a nurse alone
Heart of scarab
Blackcloaked arab
Heart of green
Humpbacked lean
Heart of wealth
Watery health
From sweet to obscene
Bubble hell broth
To thy Queen
From black to gold
Fortunes told

Old Iron man

Golden Chest Axe

In the Pan

CASABLANCA as time goes by

You must remember this……

A kiss is just a kiss

A hand upon your thigh. The fundamentalists are nigh as time goes buy.

It's still the same ole story. It's me. A fight for love and glory. Mannis. A case of do or die. Unspoken for a year writing my insides out for you here in my desert den. Closer all the time. I am closer. Violence is always with us.

The world will always welcome lovers as time goes by.

Tristan and Isolde

Mannis and Ismail

Hamlet and Ophelia

Romeo and Juliet

Willie and Maud

Bonnie and Clyde

Burton and Taylor

Paul and Joanna

Maeve and Ayill

Fred and Rosemary

Myra and Peter

Woman needs man and man must have his mate.

Ismail takes me to a hammam and hands me over to the women for safe keeping. They will wash me cleanse and massage me and sew me up with mint tea. Feel so high after this cleansing so pure fresh clean. Killing machine.

I sit in the steamwet furnace stoked by huge fullfleshed

devilwomen.

TSSSSS….. hissing heat and beaten with birch leaves to free up this skin I'm in. Hotter and hotter as the sweat dripdries out of me. I stare ahead at the naked bodies around me. Nudes. Women talking at ease in their notsosinful lifegiving skin while men in cold showers acnehours have a skinful of punishing penis envy. But here women's insides are out there in nature. Equal in their bodydoubles. Laughing and sharing. Only a woman or a girl like me can see because add the man to the frying pan and all change. A duel and the fire fuels.

The steam rises twists and swirls around this mosaic muffled world and I see the not-so-old man calling to me.

Mannis I love you. When two spirits meet and mingle why not mine with thine?

He is withered then young his beadyblue eyes beam into me and he is walking towards me trying to touch me. My foot. One touch too much.

No!

Mannis it's all right.

The women take me out of the steamsweat room and put me under the cold shower spray. Like a waterfall of light. The apparition past.

Cold shower. Hot steam. Some say the world will end in fire some say in ice I think I know enough of desire to say that ice would suffice.

My poor pores opening letting the grimedirt slide out into the vaporous hellhole. Closing my eyes I see the wooden dhows and wooden nails banged into the Pigman's fingers. I see his oozing flesh coming at me.

You are an angel I will do anything for you.

He reaches for the knife to cut off my breast. Punishing my outsides for his in.

Is this a dagger I see before me?

Mannis!

Stop! It's all right Mannis

No No No Will all the perfumes of Arabia...No incense no myrrh...?

The women burn frankincense to bring me sense. They dress me in a white robe and float the smoke under my dress up and out through my batsleeves. Jesus like.

The Pigman is bleeding and who would have thought the not-so-old man to have so much blood in him.

I wait in my steamyworld for the third. Everything comes in threes. He will come Jacob Marley ball and chain clunking through the ghostsmoke to visit me Scrooge. Mean tight lipped me for not giving them my sinskin. Must learn my lesson. The steamdream of the Green Sculptor man pressure cooker hiss pissed.

LET OFF STEAM, lose one's inhibitions, give vent to one's feelings, let oneself go.

LET GO.

The steam wraps its wet cloying hand-job dreams around me and I feel the strong viper-vapour hands tighten round my neck.

LET GO!

The heat is unbearable I cannot breathe. I look at the other nuderude bodies women curved and shaped and sculptured by nature's wetclay and the big fat man's hand thumbprints deeply poking into the tempting smooth plastered off perfection. The desire to stick your finger into the finished wedding cake and spoil all the toil. To smash the baby's brains out. Paradise lost. To chop the head off roses. To mug and rape the old lady.

Vaporous men leave me be.

Let be.

I emerge into Moroccan light tingling dusk. Scrooge on Christmas day. Generous of spirit. Visitations from the Father the Son and the not-so-Holy Ghost. Hamammed. Sipping mint tea in the cool Casablanca air. We'll always have Paris and play it again Sam and again and again. Bogart and Bacall. Love is all but passion must die and never win. Dump it in the sinbin.

You must remember this. A kiss is just a kiss.

Said The Pigman

A sigh is just a sigh

Ismail kisses my neck urgent passionate

I want inside you.

And outside my singing head I can hear the piano playing

The fundamental things apply as time goes by.

3 WISHES 3 HEARTS 3 APPARITIONS

3 X3 is 9

THE TAXIMAN

I have to leave you but I find you in Essaouira. You go with driver is good man. He no speak French no Arabic Berber Waha? Trust Me It's for your own good. The police they chase me but if they find you. You dead in jail forever. No key. Forever.

OK

Trust me I love you.

It's still the same old story a fight for love and glory a case of do or die....

We hold each other not for too long. In public. The driver is roundfaced sunhead smiling from ear to Cheshire cat ear. We set off heading for Essaouira and the closer I get the larger things become. This desert slow horizon holds me in its great palm. Space to find ourselves again. I gaze far into the horizon sizing it up. Not close up but far away. Deep and wide as oceans. A chance to see far further than before. Memory reeling me back in. City clutter spit sputtered away in my deserted shutter time. Every grain of sand a universe. Horizon gazing. Here in the desert. Unspoken me. I can see my childhood like yesterday. Smell the bluebells. Feel the blackberry squashed in my black-red juiced hands. See my world at the bottom of my bed.

Do you know where you're going to?

Do you like the things that life is showing you where are you going to?

Do you know?

Speeding through rocks and dust. Rusty car lusting towards its destination. Tired tyres of my rubber heart. The driver smiles at me in the mirror. He no speak Arabic. No French only Berber. He good man. And we do need a few good men. We drive through the High Atlas. Hair pin bending nerves standing on end as he drives faster and faster up these majestic mountains. Danger hidden deep in this Haut Atlas splendour. Atlas holding up the world. My treasure chests nestled beside me as my heart pumps faster and faster heading towards disaster.

Please slow down!

He looks at me like I'm some clown. He no understand. I lean forward pointing to the handbrake and he turns to look at me. The car speeds towards the cliff edge and I push his leg on the brake as he turns the wheel. We skid and swerve missing the edge of life by an inch and it's a cinch to die.

We drive on and on and on until we reach a small village. Tajines light up the road like a welcome home. Earthy clay pot chimneys dotted along this hungry runway. Burning bright oven-light running away with warmth and food for each cluster of limbs. A nourishing sight.

For the skin I'm in.

My Berber friend stops and shows me inside an old rundown shack.

My home

One, two, three, four. A score of children running over the mandarin peeled moon. Running towards runaway me. Pulling and kissing me and the stronger they love the bolder I become. They take my shoes off. Rub my feet with oils feed me bread and eggs and coffee. No common words just touch. Tingles mingle with my full fine feeling. Our eyes dance and whirl each other around the room. I feel elegant and pure as they dip me in their loving dance. A welcome break. My hearts at stake. They hug me tight as that night when I couldn't let go. We head for the car and my piedpiper childtail tries to search my treasure chest.

Where's the key? Where's the key?

And the key is in the Houdini heart wrapped round my neck. They cannot find my buried hearts. I let them touch the outside jewels. Ruby. Sapphire. Diamonds. Precious stones. Precious childhands. Tiny beautiful and fragile. They kiss me goodbye a thousand times and each xxx is engraved on my molesoul. I turn and smile. Children's teeth a mile long stay in my nighteyes as my easteregghead driver takes off again and the faster you go the younger you become. The deeper the kiss the longer you miss.

Right right through the night in and out of sleep…

Ain't it just like the night to play tricks when you're trying to be so quiet. We sit here stranded though we're all doing our best to deny it.

Empty road. On the road my beaming round Berber and me. Heading for the waterfalls. Not long now as I dream of touching my Prince's skin. Sawn off me. Ready to trigger the bullet balled pellets. Shooting up inside me and never coming out. Shooting right up towards a new angel life. Birthing me. Born free again.

Into darkness. Blanket desert blue-black sky perforated dartshot light. Stars yearning for another to join the busting cluster. Sleep descends upon me and I dream of war. Nuclear. Desolate. Final. Armageddon. Battling tribes. Rattling vibes. Lush greenlands turned to desert. My Mum and my Dad buried in the rubble. I scratch and scrap to dig them out. Digging further down they fall.

Nooo!!

I jolt forward as the car speeds on and ain't that just like the night to play tricks when you're trying to be so quiet.

Dawning yawning desert yellow sunegged morning. We eat eggs. That yellow life that brings in the day. Equally yoked my eggheaded Berber fried friend and scrambled me. We reach the waterfalls. Fallen angels survived the dunnest night. Driving with all our might. Poached morning stolen from our night's pain. The Cascade d'Ouzoud cascading water gushing through our frowning selves. We cannot speak. Tongue-tied us in this babbling world.

Babel Babel toil and trouble.

Babbling brook of guttural drops. Cascading foam light vowelled together in a wet release. Rainbow slicing clearcut eloquence arching through the crashing water. Bodysound surround. Technicolor understanding appears and disappears. And the waterfall fools us for a while that we all belong together. Falling from grace but Babel builds upwards.

Language upon language. A Greek Cyrillic seeking a Sikh turbaned urban beat cheating the Alpha Bravo Romeo Foxtrotting all the way to Juliet's balcony in the sky. Scraping the sound barrel and God warned us what would happen if we tried to build a ladder to the sky. One language towering high. Money mute paperplastic blueberry pie in the sky. Blown up dollarpile tickertaping around the not-so-big apple crumbled city. Money talks but it don't sing and dance and it don't walk. Crippled argot battling with our twinselves. Schizophrenic epidemic. Struck down twins. Babbling towers of wealthy power. Stealthy bombers invading our night sleep. Suicide is minor. Divide our tongues cut out our tart hearts. Punished for building castles of custard honey money into the sky. Peeping at our maker. On a different plain. On your plane?

I climb down to the Cascades d'Ouzoud the rushing water clears my ears rinsing my fears fresh. Tears left behind in my green mind. I sit on a rock. I choose the nearest to the falls. Most isolated stepping stone alone. For a while I watch an African boy dive off high rocks. Beauty shocks ripple around his black sealskin. He comes up for air spouting whale water everywhere. Headshaking seabed quaking lifeforce. He climbs up onto my rock and sits squatting beside me. We watch the water fall. I feel the tiny hint of waterglints spray on my hayskin and win the day from me.

IT'S ALWAYS OURSELVES WE FIND AT THE SEA

The waves wave at me. I smell the sea. Sand dunes wave upon wave of golden sun-surf. After an epic journey through sand and mountain we arrive here at the sea. A damp disturbing wind spins and blows across the Atlantic and feeds into my aching bones. It's black night as the taxi sputters into town and Ismail is waiting for me. As he said he would right on cue. My leading man with all the right lines.

The Desert Prince and I duck and dive in and out of ubiquitous uncle's carpet shops. Dangerous here by the sea as the police are undercover everywhere. False guides. I follow Ismail ten paces behind like all good wives. Fundamentally yours. Follow him through a dead-down part of town. Rastafarian police pursue us. Undercover cops in the guise of the weed-inhalers. Danger on every corner. We arrive inside a villa courtyard. Outside so plain-jane but these Moroccans clever in their ways they save all the pleasure for inside. Not out. Green plants spewing forth bohemian light filtering through the slatted bamboo roof. African music and eau de vie and hands warm and everywhere knocked out the cold driven into my bones. Bones old old buried bones. He kept his promise as I did mine.

I like you very much.

I touch his black head in our bedworld.

In my hands desert sands.

The moon rolls across my back

Stars move between my legs

Begging for the sky to fall

Into my arms

The sand folds beneath me
Curves form around me
Wrapped in warm hands
Penetrate nightsands
Shooting stars inside me
Shredding skin
Come within
Come inside me

MOONDIPPING

Strip: disrobe, unclothe, undress, peel, pare, skin, excoriate, take away, dispossess of, deprive of, confiscate, take apart, take to pieces, clear out, empty out, plunder, ransack, rob.

Clothes off. Naked as the day we were born. The Desert Prince and I easing into Essaouira ecstasy sea. The drops of moondust sparkle in the sea 'tween you and me. You hardsmooth skin solidcock rocked inside me. My gemstem. Touching skin goosepimpled tight bright. The fresh cold fish Atlantic water stars glint into me. Phosphorous phantoms. A skinful of this glitter splitting my soul into aching atoms. Big bang crack snackle plop. Droppings of light dancing from pore to pore cleansing my sore aching parts.

THE BIG BANG

Wave after wave of bodycrave release. Blood pumping five times faster beat beat beating the pain. And here I come again over and over four leaf clover. Multiple mayhem. African Queen split into millions of pieces hurled all the Milky Way. Four leaf clover coming all over. Tidal wave after wave shot through dandelion heated me. Blow. What's the time? Blow can't be a crime. Blow and I'm gone. Blown away.

Tantric Atlantic
Floating in the new world
A speck of dust
Bobbing up and down
Starfish clown in a starry-eyed crowd
Crowded rowdy nightnight sky
Washed up on the shore

Dryland

Creamy atomsplit me. Spilt milk bottle. White smashed shards tinkle in my whiterainbow wet bed.

Flipping in my spilt milk freshfish

All out of water out cold

Gillblocked shivering.

Hold me!

He does my desert Prince as I shake and moan coldboned alone serial killer shark. He squeezes tighter I feel lighter and the faster you go the smaller things become. The tighter he holds the bolder I become. Many powers. A lover and a fighter me and just like eecummings said in those delicious small letters

whatever we lose like a you or a me
it's always ourselves we find at the sea.

BLACK WIDOW LOST IN SAHARA

Police are continuing their investigation into the whereabouts of Mannis Poor, performance artist. She is wanted in connection with the disappearance of Gerard Serre the oil baron millionaire. The police would also like to question her following the disappearance of Irish sculptor, Donal O'Hussey and Salah De Souki, an Egyptian hotel manager who was reported missing in Oman a few months ago. She is believed to be disguised as a native Berber woman and has dyed her hair black. The police are liaising with Interpol but difficulties have arisen regarding access to the Algerian border where it is believed she may be hiding out. The investigation continues.

IRISH LOCK IN

I use ash heat and oranges for the flaming tower and greens and browns for the Irish bog. As my hands work I draw a man and woman making love by the fire. Fiddles string my memories back back to the Irish lock in nights…

Fiddly lilting lifting memories in our whisky filled souls-the noble call-each person does a turn, be it poem, song or dance. Our actress, Jella, a petite Australian girl with the voice of an angel sings Motherless Child-I can still hear her voice echoing, ricocheting off these cave walls.

Sometimes I feel like a Moooootherless child…a long way from home…

Lost Mother. Lost the root. Deracinated rancid child.

Not Mother and Lamb toy covered without joy then lowered into a box as the trolley is wheeled out of the hospice secretly shhhh… don't tell. The disappearing women trick-Where did she go? As the Sister says-It will be alright like I lost a tooth or a netball match. Not a Mother.

Titian flames licking lapping the damp cottage walls-my very own Frenchman come to take care of us. Crafting sensations each night-lean muscular body, kind cobalt eyes, blue like mine-my twin-my Plato lost half-we envelop each other- pearl pale nudes in the fairy cottage. The night of all nights.9/11 Eve. Your hands, deft as a drummer, bashing out tasty treats for us hungry actors-until we are here alone. The drum beat slows. The circus has left. You scoop out mushrooms to fill with delicious delights. Such love radiates from your hands. The whiff of garlic and scent of herbs permeates my golden skin. Your flamenco fingers fly across me, intent on perfect pitch, delivering dexterous darts of joy. Flourished from the earth. Nature's man. One touch and the fire, the food, the body all spring to life as nature intended. Your love melting me down as the bog wood turns pumpkin gold. Our crimson fire love thumping hard like the best rocksong you ever heard. We cling to each other. Bacon nudes on 9/11 Eve-before the world would never be the same and our paradise lost.

TERROR SEX

Twin Towers. That was the problem. I had the tower I needed. I didn't need another but the Irish actor playing WB Yeats just wouldn't, couldn't separate art from life. Banging on my hotel door each night looking to empty that deadly load just at those 16 men were triggering human missiles into those unsuspecting towers. Terror sex they call it.

Coined in a Salon article published ten days after the attack, "terror sex" was a kind of urgent, unguarded, end-of-the-world coitus inspired by that day's sudden jolt of uncertainty and fear.

It's biology at work—gotta procreate if the world is coming to an end. As Artaud that crazy lovable madmen who roamed Ireland with his Mexican stick proclaimed…

We are not free and the sky can still fall on our heads at any minute. Theatre was made to teach us this.

That's exactly what happened on 9/11-the sky fell on my head and I joined the New Yorkers who were having terror sex. Only I was nowhere near that flaming tower but as us girls know these flaming towers are everywhere.

That day I was driving through the West of Ireland living in that tiny fairywood cottage with only bog water to drink and a knackered ageing Aga. At the garage by the River Boyle Patrick, the mechanic lifts his head from under the car bonnet, face splashed with oil.

They crashed into the Twin Towers gurleen.

His accent is think and strong. Guinness and black treacle. I assume it is a plane crash. An accident. When I turn on the radio back at the cottage I hear the Irish man saying the world will never be the same-it's like each word has capitals the way he says it. I text a friend in England.

What's going on?

Planes crashing everywhere.

Is it being done on purpose?

Yes. All being done on purpose.

My legs feel wobbly. I feel sick and stare at last night's fire. I remember the couple in Raymond Brigg's When the Wind Blows as I fill my tin kettle and put it on the stove. It'll be alright duc' they say to each other.

Let's have a cuppa tea duc' The cake! The cake!

I am alone here since the cast left. Alone playing Maud Gonne Macbride with Shane, a horny moody Irish actor playing Yeats. He is in Dublin with his new wife and baby. He has already tried to have sex with me and I have said No. We have a long tour ahead and it would complicate things besides I didn't fancy him. He got carried away the night we went skinny dipping on Clare Island after our mindblowing opening performance and a tonne of Jack Daniels. Naked in the water with the stars aligning above Maud and Willy-he spent the night banging on my bedroom door until it was fit to break-being rejected by Maud was getting to Shane.

So here I am again on my own-I walk to the local pub .A few bulbous cherry- balloon faced men prop up the bar.

You alright gurleen?

I look at the screen and a tower, two towers are on fire-people are jumping out the windows and it seems that hijackers are flying planes into the building one after another. Babel burning.

You'll be fine here gurleen. Nothing can happen to you here.

I suddenly feel glad Shane is coming to the house tonight from Dublin. I go home and attempt to light the fire. Seamus the local farmer told me it is hard to light since the chimney is not straight. Straight towers, bent ones, flaming ones. Seamus sometimes comes around to help me with things-lots of unmarried farmers here as all the girls have fled to the city to hear the Celtic tiger roar. As I blow on the small struggling embers I feel shocked, numbed and sad that the world is not going to be the same-I was enjoying it.

There is a knock on the door and Shane is standing there leather jacket, usual scowl, fag in hand. It is a relief to have some company and he doesn't seem at all bothered by the falling towers.

They bloody deserved it-capitalist scum.

He has brought some grass with him-we smoke a lot as we do a line run. Strange combination. One almost cancels out another but we get there in the end. We sleep in separate rooms upstairs. I am freezing -the house offers cold comfort.

I'm cold.

says Jack the Lad.

Why don't you come and keep me warm?

No thanks.

Oh come on its freezing!

Though it was only September he was right, the house was damp, cold and slightly eerie since the Virgin Mary caught fire and burnt the shed down. The whole shed went up adding fuel to the fire for the local gossips who think us actors are having satanic orgies up here.

The following night we did the play to a surprisingly packed house in Castlebar and people laughed in odd places. Terror laughter

I suppose. It was fitting playing a terrorist as the US declared war on terror. Afterwards we went to the pub, the drunken tank and drank all the drinks audience members lined up for us when a man, tall distinguished and handsome kissed my hand.

May I say what a fantastic performance that was-stunning. You are extremely gifted at evoking emotions.

May I take you to dinner?

You have to love these old style gents.

Turns out he was an Iraqi/Greek gynaecologist. I took his card and said I'd call. You never know when you might need a free lunch. There is such a thing believe me. Little did I know at that point just how soon I would need him. Shane and I swallowed more drinks and accolades until our heads were bursting with high fuelled post performance schbang...Slam! Bang! On we went matching each other drink for drink. Time to go back home so we load up the car and Shane buys some vodka for the journey. I knew the world wasn't the same and I didn't know what to do about it so I necked the vodka and drove like a bat out of hell through the mild, mild West-maybe the fairies could help us or the Little people. The Leprechauns. Shane and I reached the house

No-one deserves that.

Yes they did-look at everything they have done to the world.

It's like Willie and Maud in reverse-John inciting violence and I peacemaker poet.

But the people-they didn't deserve it.

I'm ten sheets to the wind now but I can take a lot. We stumble up the stairs and Shane tries the same trick.

Come and keep me warm you mad woman.

For some reason I go this time. Some reason. Some reasons-the drink-the cold-the terror. I am cold inside and out. Bluenumb cold. Numb dumb cold and tired of being a hero, tired of sleeping alone in the damp bog bed and sad. Vodka soaked chocked sad at the evil men do. I need a hug.

So I get in bed and he starts to kiss and paw me. Not the bear I want. Within seconds. Yes seconds. A New York minute. He has pushed himself inside me and released his deadly cargo. He then falls asleep immediately. No hug. Just another slug.

I lie there knowing I am pregnant, it's the middle of the month and I have had trouble before. I decide to go to Dublin in the morning in search of the morning after pill. I have to run the Macbeth auditions the next day. This is clearly the beginning of my luckystreak.

Out damned spot.

I awake the next day after heavy dreams-my skin moist, strange, sticky. Punishing apocalyptic dreams. Omens hover. People behaving like the end of days. Air full of ash blowing in the squally wind; graveyard grains choking my throat, sharp as sandpaper.

It is a cold sad grey day.

The wipers thud back and forth in an endless rhythmic reminder that the world's heart has skipped a bloody great big beat. Ireland has declared a National day of Mourning. As we drive through the dragging Bogland all Shane can say is

I don't fire blanks.

When we arrive in Dublin everything is closed including the clinic with that magic pill that stops time, beats fate, halts penetrations lifelong penance and as I read Lady Macbeth's part in search of my Macbeth I know the sky is falling on our heads and theatre is made to teach us this.

had a Wife. Where is she now?

Go forward…the pen is mightier than the sword but what is done cannot be undone.I had a crash….A massive car crash.

She has had a blow to the head.

Can she remember her lines?

I don't know she will need brain scan.

Mannis can you remember?

Who would have thought the old man to have so much blood in him.

Memory's pointbreak surfer.

The girl with the Curly red hair she was in the car when it happened she was my best friend but what is her name. Around the hospital bed stand the cast of that lucky Scottish play .

Can you remember your lines?

Even the Doctor cannot resist the irony of a troup of Macbeth players crashing on the way to the first performance. We were travelling to play on the death island Inishoirr. But the Magpie was there the shoes were on the table and the mirror had shattered the ladders had been walked under and the milk-guilt spilt.

I never did it... never killed anyone. It's all just fantasy. I never did it because a car screeched into the back of me and stopped time.

She stopped time.

I am sitting after the crash seeing myself slumped in the car the girl with the red curly hair she loves me but all I can see is the ash of the cigarette that went in a New York second. Smoked up to my fingers and my hands burning. A cartoon bump on my head. But the show must go on.

Glamis thou art and cawdor…and thou will be what thou art promised yet do I fear thy nature?

Do I fear thy nature?

All we could hear was the clicking. The clicking of my indicator. Since then many moons ago before or after the desert I do not know. Was there a child? I think I killed it in the accident.

I'll dash its brains out.

Lady M. My concussion head mashed Paddypotato red. An ambulance but on on with the show. So much blood since the accident-bleeding everyday and who would have thought the old girl to have so much blood in her. So much blood that the accident destroyed the seed in me. There was a girl from the Desert prince and I but she is dead and gone lady. And night after night I was whiter than white. Losing blood. It never stopped coming so much blood and I sleeping with the red curly haired artist with long fingers that could cope and heal and massage me back to life. In my Dracula coffin each night with no necks to bleed and big shadow dreams of bloody hands.

LEAVE WRINGING OF YOUR HANDS AND LET ME WRING YOUR HEART.

Sleeping on the theatre floor with you my love candlelit microwave dinners and cheap champagne to love another woman to be safe from the prowling purple night. Unsex me now and fill me with love. The touching and kissing of breast on breast higher than any porn quest. Exquisite ecstasy for the buds of life to be put on hold.

There is a knocking at the gate.

Liam the local lunatic smashing on the theatre door

You're the kind of whores that paint your toe nails.

There is a knocking at the gate

But the girl with the red curly hair she sent him away brave warrior who only sees in black and white.

Washed and go. The last leg. On our last legs back to the Sahara for the Burial. We drive across the Atlas highs and lows days and nights fuel pumping into my lungs from the beaten down Mercedes. Destination Rissani. The Desert Prince's hometown.

Rissani drenched sunburnt skin wrinkled heart. So close now. Ismail takes me through the market and we are greeted by a tall handsome Berber man. His cousin and king of the desert. We sit drinking tea as they plan the entry to the Algerian Sahara.

First we will take a van with Charlie Brown then camels into the dunes.

I wander though this tiny town. Ismail's distant isolated home. Feel sure and safe planted hearts nestled in my jewel case. I am covered now safe in my disguise only the eyes still show. My windows to my molesoul. We collect his ragged donkey, that low-down beast of burden turned holy with its special cargo, waiting amid the other motor-mules carrying the burden of our lives. We load the treasure into the Charlie Brown van and are accompanied by a few of Ismail's friends. Aladdin who does acrobatics in and out of the window as we roll away from the last outpost. No post now. I sit staring tranced by the nowhere space land wanting this spaceman wanting for so long this alone lone one. To see what I have done. Only now I can see. Soul-hole me.

THIRST: dying of thirst in the desert, dryness, parchedness, dehydration.

We drive to a fountain where I wash and drink as though for the first and last time. One more 'last time' as the children say. The water on my skin. Washing like a hindu. Washing this skin I'm in. Drinking up this moment. Swallowing this life. Whole. Ismail pushes my head under the spray. Like a dog. And the cleansing has begun.

Thirsting after knowledge/thirsting for revenge desire, long for, hanker after, yearn for, hunger after, lust after, covet.

The road turns to grit and gravel grovels for my hearts. Torn apart. No plant. No sprig twig just hot greysilver tar tar. The long lonely goodbye to my old mannered self. Mannis Poor. And the longer you journey the smaller you become. The drybolt metal day turns night's way and the pin prick stars pierce my sunbrown skin. I breathe well through these new pores as we lie under the weepingly right sky. Stunning white and wholly right this Berber night. The drums begin the endless thumming rhythm drumming memory reels. My Desert Prince dances with his shoulders spanning the sky. So strong so sure so old and young. A boy cub with a man's strength. They tumble and fall laugh and crawl. Cruel is the gospel. See my eyes in the metal tea cup burning cobalt gray blue of the day. And deep inside I feel an emptying of pain draining the bloodstain in my body-brain. Three beats on my drum three times they did come. Evil ken evil. My my killer I. And a drum a drum I do come.

THIS GOLDEN ROUND

The camels are angry this morning. Proud and pungent and twisted up in rope. I am hoisted up as he wails in pain tired thin camel humiliated weight of this fat-cat human race. A sound a wail a yowling howling hail of notes falling off the lamenting scale.

Everyone is up and Ismail strides alongside our camel caravan guiding us to the star. The sun is not yet cleared its dune and the softsand call is like an echo of another world. This golden round. The camel feet sink and bony legs lift in an awkward graceful rhyme as the waves of grains of specks of sand join land in land to make this golden syrup silence. This honeydripdrop calm sweetens my mind. Paradise found in a grain of sand. I understand what Jesus meant. About the mustard seed. And days and nights like this until all that's left is Ismail and I and hearts and rib. We head into the spot for the burial ground safe and sound sssshhh Sahara.

See Sahara

Be Sahara.

THE BURIAL

Black Coal burning
White light
Red fire Daybreak
Green fire
Blue fire
Gold full fire sunrise

We reach the highest dune spot. I place my hearts in a triangular trinity. Each encased in its jewelled chest from the golden axe city. In the middle I bury the rib. Eve's not Adam's. We collect the wood to start the fire watching carefully each stage to red-hot melt down. The Iron Man seems to be smiling as he considers his funeral pyre. Dancing higher.

Revenge is nigh- high on the agenda. A natural bittersweet knee jerk reaction. I am natural. Not sick. Violence is always with us now as always and Ismail and I are together in sickness and in health. He cures me with stealth and skin-wealth and with my body I thee worship.

But this ending is the cure all. The sun slants upwards towards us as the fire spurts ashes. I watch my jewelled hearts catch fire. Beauty struggling through the weeds. The Iron Man melts down until I can see his flesh underneath. His flesh ready to burn. Rotten now. Tasting no good. I bite and spit. History's whore. Bored of hate.

Black

Black as night. Witches' coven. Black African night. Black to look good. Black heart. Dead coals. Charcoal black on white. Black and grained spots on my soul. I sit in darkness. Nothing nowhere girl and I strike up a light. A flame from the stone hearts of others. Blackskin of my desert prince. Beautiful smoothsight. Bruisedhearted others. Blacken my world with your violent eclipse. Your drunken dark souls.

White

Born stunning white and wholly right. Whitewashing ablutio baptisma. White not pink or flesh coloured anglo red skins. White where all colours light and reunite. Body white resurrects the many colours. Cloudpuff white.Rainbow white. White light from the black Ironman coal. The badluck peacock tail. The silver moon condition. Almost daybreak but not quite.

Red

Red rag to a bull. Reds under your beds. There in the fire. Lady in red. Dangerous head. Red for stop green for go. Red blood from the hearts of others. Blue blood of the not-so-old man. Royal rich oil blood pumping through our lucky Western veins. Speed and wind in our hair. Lead in their pencils. Red sunset. Sunrise daybreak in the dry cold desert night. Aching for the sun that you wish you could eat at its hottest core. Sore winged Icarus wingbeaten. Moth spirit unbroken. Flying at the light again and again and that fat old sun in the sky shines on and on till the end of time. Crazy diamond yellow hot pie.

Green

Green for go. The fire lights up green tips. Greenfingers for a garden of hopeful Eden. Sinless. Skinless. Green as the fresh cut grass. Emerald city green on the Ireland Isle. Beauty and its beast. Green with envy Oh! that masterful green-eyed monster. Jealous love kills the goldfire green flame. Dissolves into black coal. Stars.

Stars and all else dead coals.

Blue

Bluc. Gasblue. Pure blue. Skyblue. My eye blue. Ocean blue lingers in your wintermind. Seethrough eyetrue blue. Piercing right to our inside souls. Twinkle light sharp eyes staring from my old brown face.

Your eyes, Mannis, are jewels in the crown. Blue flickers lift our blue soul holes.

Gold

Gold. The alchemist's rainbow ending. Dream come true. Rolled gold heat to treat us to a hotwater bottle night. The gold in the daisy white egg yoked fertile glory. Gold dust.

A Butterfly arrives upon us out of the gold fire pyre from nowhere. Must be somewhere and as always there is magic.

But hate we must. A monument to my pain. Mannis made. Manned by a girl.

Tis Time for his serenade.

Rib of birthdead babebone
Ditch-delivered by a nurse alone
Heart of scarab
Blackcloaked arab
Heart of green
Humpbacked lean
Heart of wealth
Watery health
From sweet to obscene
Bubble hell broth
To thy Queen

From black to gold
Fortunes told
Old Iron man
Golden chest axe
In the pan

I am the devourer and the redeemer. The Desert Prince and I lie here on the rockstone. Alone. Before we strike. Fire. Lovers entwined prima materia and natura abscondita. Body and soul. In the silver moon condition androgynous deity hovering between male serpent sun and female serpent moon. The snake snakes between us licking us inside out. It has us licked.

Around us I have drawn a triangle within it a square within it a circle. Squaring off the circle to make the two sexes one.

All things do live in three but in the four they merry be.

Opus alchymicum

We lie near the tree bidden fruit

Fructus arboris immortalis

A heart at each point in my chothonic trinity daemon trinus. This is the key to the treasure house. Three-headed monster grows if we eat from the tree. The tree head hearts buried here. The Iron Man awaiting his white dove release from this Queen of Sheba.

He is the Holy Ghost. His fire unites the Father and son of man not-so-kind. The rib under me. The bodies swollen in my whale belly. Warmth of incubation brooding.

But before the fire we need the water.

The Scarab 1 2 3

Unigenita only begotten born of itself beheaded and dismembered sun-beetle.

Heart of Scarab

Chopped up until his head is golden and body is salt white. The third unicorned.

Nulla aqua fit elixir nisi illa quae fit de scarabaeis aquae nostrae.

No water will become the elixir save that which comes from the scarabs of our water.

Drink the scarab potion in preparation for 3 x 3. Waiting incubating vision heat so intense that the hero loses his hair. Baby born again. From the funeral pyre the winged old man raised higher and higher out of his chest a white dove.

Rak A Tak

Ismail starts to drum drum away the night. Starlight I lie and starstare upwards as I start to write.

Just coz I am a girl I suppose you think…no….I need to start tonight. Start to get it all down. Now I have this pen I am mightier than the sword.

Write to someone the story of a serial killer.

She seemed such a nice girl. Straight from a loving family. Can't be her. TV search continues with the slime making headlines. Writing. Waiting for the dawn. Handheart aching. Dawning yawning it'll be easier in the morning. Cold desert wrapped up warm in his arms as I feel the gold sands lose their blackness. Firegold turned blueashen red embers flickering away. The fat old sun starts to rise from cold blue chill to greenred Bedouin bed. I can rest now… nearly at my last syllable of recorded time. Bonewarmed and buried pain. My heart pumps again. Pumping life into my honeysmile. I smile a smile as generous and wide as the Arabian crescent moon falling on its back.

THE LOVE MAKING

Making Love

We set up homecamp in the centre of the triangular burial ground. Madonna and child to come in the middle of the trinity. Ismail and I lie naked in the loving sand. Inside out with love. He caresses this skin I'm in licking me from crown to top-toe smoothing away the direst cruelty. He comes close to my honeysmile lightly licking the inside out. My body spasms in wanting needing more inside than out but he withdraws his tongue and touches my breasts aching moons of fleshjoy of livewomanhood and here I am now on the brink from girl to woman. *Please inside me.* And he pushes the tip of his rock lock stock and barrel full force in just a little then out. Want you inside me. He speaks in my ear a language I do not know and I am cleansed of my past national paindrain.Colours.Flags mean nothing here in the sandy blank white. All colours now one. Flags of blood red and mean blue long forgotten.

And the error bred in the bone of each man and woman craves what it cannot have not universal love but to be loved alone.

Loving me here alone. No-one to steal me away from my self. Open mind. Open legs. No secrets here. Please. Come inside me.

So there are the summers. The ones in the beginning and the ones in the end. I am beginning and ending in the summer from gold to gold.

From black to gold and gold to black. A month of days and nights. None months of moons and suns. The sun spins and weaves this blackearth us into gold. Creation's spinning Jenny rays. Spun into the earth. Mercury rising to meet the sungod. And for much more than 4O days and 40 nights we lie in triangular love. Juiced in desert days. Food delivered from the tree. Eaten unbanished me.

It is spring now and I am pregnant with child full of the seeds ploughed and scattered. We await the pink flamingos who drink at the oasis. A mass of pink flight out of the desert night. One-legged fragility. I remember it well. But I am strong now bones and skin shining in the mirror of his eyes. Unspoken me ready to bury the past. An eye for an eye is blindness so I am hoping after this I can see again. Identity disappear the eye of the other gone here.

Love scene not obscene. Sandground here in the present continuous. 3 x 3 is 9 and 9 months of stroking. Loving. Giving. Baby boygirl.

Waters breaking

Flushing rinsing gushing through my brown straw-kissed body and soul and from the heat comes the oceans of the world between my legs from inside out. Wave after wave of pain in the rain. Screaming to the stars and he holds me tighter. Flamingos rise up in flight heading for the pink golden sun. Strawberry blond light. The faster the painwave comes the smaller I become. And this is coming.

Bigger than my insides. Coming out. This Life.

I'm a woman now or soon will be. Who will visit me ? 3 wise women ? 3 kings? Will there be kings in 3 days? 3 years? 300? 3000? Will we be here? I hear the first cry from my insides and out we both come. My new born babe comes out. Flushing. We come ready now. Gushing for this life. Rushing. For better or for worse. She is coming to you. She is coming. In hunger or thunder. In wind or rain. Inside and out. In love. In hate. In highs and lows. In rainbows. In full moondraining beauty. In shining magpie searching chance. This life is coming and is beginning and ending in the summer.

I'm living it
And so my precious darling
So are you.

PRECIOUS CARGO

So precious these small limbs, stones and bones. I am in charge of this wondrous cargo-pearly white teeth glinting in the licoricey night-so many moons in her magical mouth. I must keep her safe. I am the women at the mouth of the cave. Fear runs through my veins, this mother fear so clear. Must keep her safe. Safe and sound. Safe as houses. Sleep tight don't let the bed bugs bite or the Monster's mighty member smash up your life. It is time. No more travels-time to go back to stone and bone-to the top of the world. Ismail urges me to go south. He has word that the police are coming. He says he will find me when the coast is clear. But there is no coast. It feels wrong to part and split this holy trinity but he insists I am in danger and need to move on. He will always find me he says. See Sahara. Be Sahara.

The desire extinguished by birth. Belly bloated body been a carrier for nine months-now no longer body of desire on fire. Motherhood-what a blast-shedding your skin and transforming yourself to birth anew. A reallife reincarnation. The long road of constant glares now nowhere.

As night's comfort wraps us into the desert sand, stars our lamps, you stare deep inside me- deep pools of curious love.

I will call you Indunn-newly born.

BABY ON MY BACK

Some say the world will end in fire some say in ice. I think I know enough of desire to say that ice will suffice. The heat burns me up. I dream of ice, ice, ice.

I take this little parcel on my back a reallive backpack to care for. Ismail says I am to stay with the Dogon tribe further down south. They have small caves and tiny huts in the side of the mountains where we can hide away. Tucked into the earth.

Close to nightfall a man in a blue veil appears-as tall as the stars-waves and waves of deepseas billow around him- only his eyes flash indigo black.

He is a Tuarag man. They are known as the Blue people. The Blueman gives Indunn a tiny flute made from wood. He takes my hand and lifts me and baby up on the camel.

A violent midnight sky drags us through the night-softswollen sands soothe our rhythmic walk. The Tuarag strides gigantic towards the see-far women.The women sing songs as the drum beats shudder the nightsands. The men sit high on the camel's back circling the women as they sing. I watch this goldenblue whirligig. A star shatters over our head splitting the sky. A torchbearer to guide us home. The Blueman tells me it is the Sirius star.

These see-far women's voices mesmerise us. Baby and me. One love.

The Tuarag leads me to an oasis. I bathe baby as the drum beats scatter her cries. Jurassic thirst quenched.

Indunn's breath brands tiny footprints on my heart.
Breathe.
Keep breathing.

MIRROR MIRROR

Mirage-rooted in mirror. Latin *mirari* -to look at in wonderment.

At the oasis I splash my face and I see babygirl in the reflection. That damned reflection shouting back at us.

BE GONE!

My very own little Tarzan girl untouched by Western greed quest where the mirror is everywhere-iphone, youphone, mephone-instagram tram of filter delights. This pageantry of vanity. Everyone a celebrity-look at me, my dinner, my eyes, my insides. Look at my skin shine. Look at my skin shine. I am I am I am beautifully alive. Here I am on my private silver screen languishing in my limey light. I am preening peacock alive. My very own TV channel. All about Eve. More than 15 minutes Andy so much more than we bargained for.

Narcissus nightmare- *narcissism* denotes an excessive degree of self-esteem or self-involvement, a condition that is usually a form of emotional immaturity.

Echo could not live outside of her desire for Narcissus. Echo had not enough ego, and Narcissus far too much.

Young girls arrested by their very own beauty- poleaxed at the alters of their reflection-stunned goddesses stymied by a myriad of possible selves-soon to freeze forever on those cyber pages.

Frozen male-gaze girls echoing through time.

Who shall I be? A pretty girl, doll-like dress-up innocent girl, pigtails and snails girl, pussycat doll-like riot girl. Wild girl, nurse girl, riding red girl, Madonna/whore girl, nice girl, which girl? Bitch girl. Pouting lips want to kiss girl. Boobs pulled up to my chin girl.

Lean too far forward so we can watch you drown girl.

A witch hunt all the same but now the women can drown themselves and not even make a ripple.

Perfect.

Western girls too unfurled they say.

Shut her up in a box girl. Cover her cover girl. Wrap her up tight-scarfed girl.

That's better.

Wonka's everlasting gobstopper girl- more more moorish indulgence beyond belief and world's whimpering end makes you feel slightly sick, a Macdonalds wolfed down in a slystolen minute-riding high on the rollercoaster ride of disappointment. Shiny burger salivating your insides until the rotten chemical carcass mutates and drives its filthy cargo right through your mutinous immune system.

And more cows die on this scorched land.

And the forests burn.

Time to go back to the Earth- plants, fruits and nuts …

Back to the future.

I lift her onto my back as we approach the water -my dolphin girl. Electric currents run through us. Jump my girl jump and dive in the water-flipping and gliding from here to eternity.

We shall slide to Iceland my love.

We shall stay out all night, doors and hearts open no lustful heat to beat our bruised bodies.

I will sculpt in ice.

Iron man dead and buried.

Ice will suffice.

HELJA AND THE UNDERWORLD

We need to hide my love. Dive down to the coldest place on earth. Fata Morgana- the superior mirage in the polar region where dancing spikes and towers appear to float in the sky.

Icicles drip in my ears.

Helja the Icelandic goddess appears- half beautiful and half a decaying blue rotting corpse with bones growing outside of her body.

Smash! Crack! Whack-each hammering whack breaking my icy heart. Lizzie Bordcn with her axe.40 whacks. Only the purest ice can be used-razor sharp chisels slice and shape Helja. I will carve out my place in history.

Welcome to Haljo concealed place under the world.

Underworld.

I'll sculpt from ice this time hacking away at the raw block -master of my creation. Hammer and pick. Stoneage tools, hand-axe and a razor sharp love sculpting the icy blue bones outside her body.

In the cool cave I shall build my own underworld.

3x3 is 9.

9 caves in Helja-for the 9 stages of the soul until re-birth.

IT TAKES A VILLAGE…

Horizon wobble heat greets the new dawn. Indunn's morning yawning wonder awakens the yellow plains ahead.A maze of huts, cones, prisms, cylinders rise up behind the baobab trees. High above us grottoes tucked inside the sandstone cliffs dance playfully. Little huts topped off with a witches hat. Grottoes. Sounds like Santa might be inside.

Land of the Dogons where they bury the dead.

All human life began in this rock shelter.

The Turag man sits with us as the Dogon women bring us food and water. They teach us some Dogon words- eat, fire, sleep-the words you need to survive. I draw what I see in the sand or sketch in my book. They take me to make pots in the female granary. It's nice to stay there with the women and make my pots and mini figures. Indunn likes them. I can tell.

A Dogon women sews together a patchwork quilt for our cave-she hums a tribal tune. Another woman starts to play an eerie melody-Indunn's elphin face screws and scrunches-so changeable in its pale alabaster hue-the whole of the sky and the whole of my heart shudder and shiver with love.

Fire and Ice. That's the game today. Putting our hands in fire and ice. Which is worse ?

Which story is more painful?

I show Indunn a map of the world and draw a line for our route from Africa to Iceland. It's time to go. I write on a piece of paper and I imagine her soft voice-void of contempt, cherished cadences of a child's voice.

Some say the world will end in fire…some say in ice. I think I know enough of desire to say that ice will suffice.

We will travel to the top of the world-she spins our little grapefruit globe in her hand and points at Iceland.

I nod. Yes. I draw Ran the mermaid goddess and we pretend to swim on the sand getting it in our eyes and mouths-laughing until we cannot breath and then we see the cut girls walk past with their missing parts. Such stories we tell. Some are so dangerous. How can they cut off such pleasure before it is even known. How scared they must be these cut girls.

The sun drops heavily switching off day. I watch it leave, giving way to night's uncertain ceiling. Indunn sleeps on my chest. Sunset red head child's golden slumber as the Sirius star dazzles behind her.

THE DOG DAYS

The sky is alive with so many stars- but one star, Sirius gleams like a goddess -no one knows how the Dogons know so much about this star-you don't always need books to learn.

The ancient Greeks observed that the appearance of Sirius heralded the hot and dry summer and feared that it caused plants to wilt, men to weaken, and women to become aroused. Due to its brightness, Sirius twinkles more in the unsettled weather conditions of early summer. To Greek observers, this signified certain emanations which caused its malignant influence. Anyone suffering its effects was said to be "star-struck" *(ἀστροβόλητος, astrobólētos)*. It was described as "burning" or "flaming" in literature. Poets at the heart of what matters.

Sirius is known as the Dog star bringing heat, drought, storms, lethargy, fever. The season following the star's reappearance came to be known as the "dog days". A period marked by lethargy, inactivity or indolence.

My dog days sit heavy on me barking out my lost desires. Heatsilt pulling me down into the earth-suffocation melts me into sand. Blood floods between my legs hotheat release from the pricklingpain. I stare as the sand turns as red as Sirius. The women come and take me into the red tent. The menstruation hut where women must go when bleeding to keep away from the men.

Unclean. Unfuckable. Undisturbed.

THE CIRCUMCISION TENT

That night we sit around the fire under the flaming star. Telling stories. Stories are danger. Stories can hurt. Stories are not innocent.

Sitting around the fire we listen.

The women settle down and tell the young girls this ancient tale that prepares them to be cut inside.

Lanududd -the elder women in the tribe washes the girls in preparation. She is the storyteller. She leads a group of young girls into a tent- silently we watch Lanududd tell her story. She moulds some clay in the shape of a woman lying on her back. This is the Earth. Then she uses a stick man to show that he wants to put his thing inside her. She jabs and jabs. She then draws a vagina and makes an ant hill with an arrow between. Amna the male God tries to enter her and the clitoris rises against him this is why it must be removed and destroyed. The male soul lies in the clitoris and must be cut out. The jackal dual soul is dangerous. Better to cut it off. Divide masculine and feminine for good.

We watch from the side seeing these young girls crying and screaming in pain. Lanududd takes one girl in her arms, threads the needle as good ol' auntie sews her up.

The dual soul is a danger; a man should be male, a woman female. Circumcision and excision are the remedy. They tell all sorts of stories and reasons for cutting girls pleasure off. The men get a kick out of a tighter hole, dry sex, less odor, less mess in fact-all sewn up - neat and tidy.

Depending on the tribe and geography as a girl you have a choice.

Type I:

Type I: is the excision (removal) of the clitoral hood with or without removal of all or part of the clitoris.

Type II: is the excision (removal) of the clitoris together with part or all of the labia minora (the inner vaginal lips).

Type III: is the excision (removal) of part or all of the external genitalia (clitoris, labia minora and labia majora) and stitching or narrowing of the vaginal opening, leaving a very small opening, about the size of a matchstick, to allow for the flow of urine and menstrual blood. The girl or woman's legs are then bound together from the hip to the ankle so she remains immobile for approximately 40 days to allow for the formation of scar tissue.

Pro-choice is FGM. Supported by stories, told by men and women alike.

Stories are dangerous.

They should have a health warning.

200 million

A vast silence hangs over these 200 million cut girls.

This unbelievable, unfathomable act against 200 million.

Us women and girls been stitched up for centuries.

Time for a different story.

How careful we who tell stories must be.

We will stitch it. We will mend it.

Beware of the stories and who is telling them. What a reason to take away desire but looking back at myself maybe it is the best way for our girl to avoid the highs and lows, the ecstasy and addiction to the orgiastic high of bodyshaking delight.

The cave mouth is beckoning – wide open- agog at the world.

I sit and think- open mouthed warrior.

Aghast.
What I have become.
We need a different story.

WOMAN AT THE MOUTH OF THE CAVE

The Dogon caves shelter us under a curved-stone sky as hard as the holes in my heart. We clamber and climb over the mud tombs inside the burial cave. Time to go deeper. Inside the earth. Cement our love. Hibernate before it's too late. We squeeze through the tiny slit hole into the inner cave and as I push and scrambled through the darkness I turn to help Indunn through and her little head emerges through the almighty rock-iridescent jewels sparkling inside-red lava ceiling and aquamarine ice. The cave walls glinting russetred. Squeeze and slide my little Indunn.

I wrap and swaddle you, wrap, wrap, wrapping terrified they will cut you. A woman tells me they cut babies as young as 20 days old, the girl's bleed on me and I wipe their red blood on the walls. Will these hands never be clean? Cave art whisper secret pictures. Castrations carnival. The woman tries to take you. They say I am unwell. I try to breatsfeed you but the sweat slips across my chest.

Your small head slides around my gigantic breast-no harden nipple for this girl arrested into Motherhood-poor slip sliding little head.

The Dogon woman keeps shoving my breast into your mouth and your little head keeps slipping around- your face so scrunched up red and angry that I delivered you unto this world and I can understand that my love for what a world it is. Where can I go to bring you into a new place another spaceface than this-riots on the streets, people scramble for a bite to eat. This summer of fires and desires you have been delivered under.

I always knew I would find Motherhood hard that's why I ran

away from it for so long, ran and ran as it chased me- screaming for its milk, but now you are my magnet. Clinging onto me for dear life. I will embrace it and lay down my life for it. I am the woman at the mouth of the cave, as the Doctor said. That doctor.

I want us to make an unknown island, not trodden on before, we can create it. A new world far from the madding crowd until they learn the secret of us.

I have seen such things. Your life will be better than mine. I swore it. With no hearts to tear out. I need to take you away from here.

I am the woman at the mouth of the cave.

You are a girl - a girl who will have boobs and periods and be able to give life and a man will always have a willy that he'll want to stick into things when it's working- we can't get away from that.

But there is still so much fun to be had. I want to stay with you forever young and when I grow little we will play in the playground and be best friends…i am you really and you are me.

We will go back to the land. Go forward. A different story. An inversed black mirror utopia. No more daunting futile apocalyptic future horror shows. No. A real place not Never-never La la Land nor fallen Eden. No fool's paradise burnt to cinders but reallife loving -laughing-living peace.

We can slide all the way to ice…land. So tired of the beating heat. Dreams of dripping icy caves. That is where we will make our home. I have a feeling... Are you ready for the ride?

BLEED AND SEED

The women come and go placing leeches on my back to drain my blood. Drain the pain.

Leaves and potions grinding all around me mortar and pestle special for the mother to spurt milk. Dried up dairygirl needs to be cured. In and out of sleep I slip further into dreams of dragonfish evolving wild for life, rapacious remorseless survivors reaching dryland as small girls bleed.

Dragonfish light up the dark. Others are drawn to their light unaware of their invisible teeth sharp as needles.

Caught in their trap. I adapt growing gills to breath blood.

Bleed and Seed.

When I awake she is gone. They tell me it is to rid her of her male soul. I do not want her to be cut. I promised that her life would be simpler than mine with no hearts to cut out.

I call a small girl to take my message to the Turagman. The Blueman to come for us. I have to get Indunn away from here… before they rid her body of its maleness.

I stare at the blank moon hearing my baby's cry-cut before life has begun. Her body grown inside to perfection, hands barely unscrunched. Your cries shake the earth. Let down. No good mother I.

I take the Tuarag's scarf and swaddle my burntbaked body. Wrapping round and round. Mummified mummy. I start to cover myself with sand and rocks-bury myself to death. Stone after stone upon me. Hot rocks and sand burn. The last chink of light blackened as I place the final crystal gem on my all seeing eye. The fight pops

out of me like an old cork.
Seasailor girl all washed up.
All is silence.

THE HORSEMAN COMETH

Theseus and the Minotaur. Will I wave the right flag?

The pale horse cometh. Death becomes her.

Black, red, white, pale horses galloping towards me echoing through time. Hooves rocking the earth.

Memory's pointbreak surfer riding waves of ancient pain.

A richred haired mermaid lashes around next to me talking of war. She is struggling to breath, struggling for air.

A grey-haired young girl is sitting by a river of plastic signing for packages as oil drips from her pen burning her alive…ashen lady lost in the big sleep

A crowblack feathered horse presses down on my breastchest, redhot hooves pierce my skin me until he flies away batwings beating into the starless sky dragging starving children in his wake.

A white horseman approaches wearing a golden crown – I reach for it and it turns to ash in my hands.

Induuuuuuunn…

I hear his voice.

Ismail rides high on his white horse-the end of time saviour to awaken me from the Big Sleep. He lifts the heavy stones off my chest and unwraps the sheets I am swaddled in - catacombic mummy buried deep.

The Desert Prince sweeps in on his steed pulling down the circumcision tent rescuing Indunn from the cutting women knives a-ready.

Kind father sent from heaven.

He holds me close. Be Sahara See Sahara.

He lifts us high on his horse as we gallop into the hungry night- man woman and child. A hopeful trinity.

We arrive at the Berber camp and lie together as the fire warms our bone and flesh. My stopgo heart now released fragile as papyrus near the flame.

Triangular love.

Ismail holds me close rubbing me back into the world. He says it isn't safe now and we should wait a while to cross to Europe. I tell him my plan to move to the icy lands. He says we will rest with the Berbers for a while before we head North.

Many are making the journey north these days so no-one will notice another woman and child following the stars.

Our dog days are over and done.

THE REMEMBERING

It is terrible how much has been forgotten which is why remembering seems such a holy thing.

There is the beginnings and the endings. There was a moment when hate was buried and the man and the woman came together as one. There were pink flamingos flying. It was here on earth and there were screeches of pain turned to love and laughter. There was rushing and gushing.

There were big ugly giant beetles in the sky spreading the sand into a duststorm covering everything. There were...helicopters. That is the name. There were helicopters kicking up the sand and we could see nothing. I could not see anything. Pure sand-wipe time took my baby.

There were loudspeakers and guns aimed at us but so much sand and the Berber woman were running forward throwing things at the giant enemy. Fruits nuts and stones. I ran and ran and didn't stop running there was no more Ismail no more Berbers no more no one just me here with the pen that is mightier than the sword.

I wait quietly buried in the sand until they have gone.

Waiting. Alone. I sit and stare feeling like Lawrence of Arabia.

I am too scared to move. For a long time I just sit and burn and cool as the days pass. Much time has passed and I have seen more than fifty moons come and go. I am weary now. Tired of death and running. Catch me if you can. I am innocent. The pen is mighty but innocence is mightier. I head down further into Africa where it did or didn't begin. Mali….Mauritania… biblical places.

THE BURIAL CAVES

After many long nights of wandering and sleeping in the sands the dry biting wind draws me back to the Dogon burial caves on the edge of the Sahara. Trees tall and stately splash green in my foreign eye. Ghosts of an old Eden waking up. Eternal wanderer of arid lands.
I follow an animist priest up the rocky trail.
Viens tu est un belled spirit. Un fille de feu.
Firefly I.
I scramble up the cliff face and peer into the cave. At the the cave entrance-I clamber and climb inside through to the inner cave. I squeeze my body through the birthing slit in the rock. Grinning skulls greet me, piles and piles of bones, shreds of clothing, and amulets and totems placed there centuries ago. I fall down as bones cover and smother me. Surrounded. Bareboned alone. She is dead and gone lady. She is dead and gone. Gonegirl. I see her blanket lying there among the bones on the cave floor and wrap it up close to me to feel my baby pearl again.
The smell of her sends me wild-eyed weeping wailing…
Inddddduuuuuuuuuuuuuuuuuuuuuuuuuuuuuuuu-unnnnnnnnnnnnnnnn!

The echo of my voice slamming back at me ricocheting loss. Alone as the world turns. Alone in the cave. Brand new ancient. Motherhood interrupted.
I sit and stare at cave paintings and imagine my little girl racing around the fire. And then I howl- all my unused voice out until my heart stops.
She has gone.
My girl.

THE BOABOB TREE

Many moons pass- I dive down into icecold memory-the geysers rise and smoke around me- I have been on the run so long even the outstretched moon looks down on me - Mannis. Man is. Man is mute.

The priest speaks in French. He brings me water, fruit and nuts.

I don't know which language to teach girl when I find her.

I need to talk to her. She deserves her mother's tongue.

The men call me Blue because of my eyes. They change with the sky-time can switch remember. Some say I'm a witch. The woman have named me the silent sculptress all that sibilance gives me a snake vibe. They'll never find me up here.

Sitting on top of a rumbling seething mass of craters.

Volcanic me ready to blow. That's where we'll go. When I find her.

The land of ice.

That will suffice.

I sit under the Baobob tree. Babapapa elephant trunk me. Over many moons I watch it transform its green velvety coat into a hard coconut-like shell.

Hard shell-mother.

Baobab is the only fruit in the world that dries naturally on its branch. Strange fruit. Strange world.

These fruits keep me alive.

Instead of dropping and spoiling, it stays on the branch and bakes in the sun for 6 months – I cannot drop and spoil. I am a mother now. Have to stay on the tree. Find her.

Harvest her.

All is harvest.

A BEDTIME STORY

On the darkest longest night I light candles in each cave then settle. The Dogon women ever watchful sit by my side. Remember stories are wild. Stories are dangerous. Just don't shoot the messenger but you usually do.

Once there was a little girl who was so very happy-she ran wild and free through the fields of her childhood home-her Mummy and Daddy loved her so very much. One day she was running in the woods with her friends when she heard the trees bending and an almighty growling echoed through the forests. There stood an almighty monster with a large protruding nose that lit up whenever he smelt children in the forest, especially girls, then his nose would get so red it might burst. That's why all the adults told the girls they should not play in the forest. When the other girls saw the monster's glowing nose, they were scared and ran home to their beds but Martha wasn't scared, she didn't want her friends to be frightened so she grabbed the biggest stick she could find and collected some rocks in her bag, she smeared her face with mud so the monster would not see her. She climbed up the highest tree and waited and waited. She swore she would kill the monster so all the girls could play freely again in the forest and become strong and brave. All night the forest was silent except for the hooting of the owl and the scurrying of the foxes. Then the earth began to shake and the monster pounded the forest floor heading straight for her. Through the darkness, she could see his bulbous red nose and the whites of his eyes and aimed her arrows right at them. Down below she had set a trap for his feet, the arrows were right on target, blinding him immediately, moments later his legs were caught in the trap. As he fell Martha showered him with stones from above. His nose shriveled up and his body fell floppy and flaccid on the forest floor.

The Monster was dead! Martha called all the girls back to the forest and they danced and cheered for now they would be safe forever and never have to worry about the monster and his big bulbous red nose again.

DOLPHIN GIRL

After many moons I begin to travel slowly back up the continent to my Burial ground in the deep desert. I must find her. My girl. I climb up a dune, the highest one I have found for many days and I am sure it is where the flamingos drink. The oasis is on the other side. As I reach the top breathing heavily I collapse and crawl to the edge looking down I see pink shimmering light upon the water. It must be the flamingo lake. I slide down the other side and fall in a heap at the bottom hair tangled up in sand. The kind face of the oldest woman is hovering over me wiping my forehead with a cool balm and I am picked up and taken to the tent. The Berber women are all around me laughing and talking, they hug me and bring me food and water. Wash me all over with their desert love.

She was born I know it she was born here. I drag them to the burial ground to show them and gesture to them rocking my arms.

Where is my baby?

I use their headscarves wrapped in a bundle to show the baby like I did as Maud in the play and then unravel the sheet to show death. They nod.

She is dead and gone lady.

The Berber women instinct is never wrong.

But were there bones? A body? I gesture to my bones-my chicken bones.

No bones. No body.

And Ismail?

They put their hands to their wrists to show the Police still have him and then to their mouths to sign that he will never betray me.

So I go from country to country, a sun blind muted wanderer alone and all the time I hear not the screams of my victims but the laughter of a young girl. Happy and free. It was me before the wave of pain. The hate and the war. In the desert I wander and search. Watching the fallen nights swell into darkness.

The Sengalese ladies bring me water and fruits from the trees. They are the most beautiful women I have ever seen. Mad-eyes lady of the low lands.
Have you seen my baby?
I come to a river after months in the desert. People have been kind and no-one has reported me to the Police. If they have the Police cannot find me. A fugitive in the desert. I sit by the river and wash my burnt skin. I see my reflection for the first time in many moons. My eyes are shining so bright. I hear the laughter of a little girl splashing, merry as can be and I think it was me before the hurt. The killing and the pain.
I dive into the water swimming underneath feeling amphibiously happy. Dolphin free. I come up for air slap bang in front of a little girl paddling in the sea with two Senegalese woman. They are strikingly beautiful but the girl looks different to them. She is brown skinned and she is only about 33 moons old. I swim nearer to her underwater and we surface together bursting and gasping for air. We shoot up and blow the sea spraying water in each other's faces. Her eyes are deep with an ever-changing palate. Just like mine. She smiles. The dolphin girl rising high splashing joy across the sky. Majestic. Beautiful. Flashing smile. A mile of happiness in one face. I see it was me. Long long ago. Miles and miles and smiles away. My soul as old as centuries. Before the parasites came to feed on my fertile flesh. Ransacking my lighthouse. Kidnapping my golden years.
Our eyes meet and I know. I am a woman not a girl.
She is alive.
Our girl.

Printed in Great Britain
by Amazon

11873799R00150